# Hockey Heroes

## John Danakas

James Lorimer & Company Ltd., Publishers
Toronto, 1998

James Lorimer & Company Ltd. acknowledges the support of the Department of Canadian Heritage and the Ontario Arts Council in the development of writing and publishing in Canada. We acknowledge the support of the Canada Council for the Arts for our publishing program.

Cover illustration: Sharif Tarabay.

**Canadian Cataloguing in Publication Data**
Danakas, John
     Hockey heroes
(Sports stories)
ISBN 1-55028-597-1 (bound) ISBN 1-55028-596-3 (pbk.)
I. Title II. Series: Sports stories (Toronto, Ont.).

PS8557.A53H63 1998    jC813'.54    C98-930348-9
PZ7.D35Ho 1998

James Lorimer & Company Ltd., Publishers
Egerton Ryerson Memorial Building
35 Britain Street
Toronto, Ontario
M5A 1R7

Printed and bound in Canada.

# Contents

*This one, with love and a hope for the brightest of futures, is for my nieces and nephews: Maria, Costa, Theo, Alexia and Giorgio.*

# 1

# Shark Attack!

Number 18, Cody Powell, left-winger for the Transcona Sharks, skated down the left flank of the ice, the puck cradled securely in the curve of his stick. As he crossed the opposing team's blue line, his legs pumped harder and his heart beat faster. Like a shark hunting nearby prey, Cody could not just see the net, but smell it. Through his helmet he could hear the thunderous cheers from the fans in the stands reverberating through Lord Strathcona Arena. He knew a goal was not far off, felt it in his thirteen-year-old bones with a confidence that guided his every move.

Out of the corner of his eye Cody spied teammate Kyle Kelley, number 9, charging the net, the tail of his long blond hair flying in the wind, his tall, muscular frame clearing an easy path in front of him. Gifted with great hockey skills, Kyle was also an extremely physical player who didn't hesitate to plow down opposing players with his superior strength and size. Kyle was the star on this team, in this league. And he looked the part, Cody thought — like a hockey card come to life. Cody was lucky to be playing on the same line with a player of Kyle's calibre, someone all the players and coaches, and even the parents, agreed would one day make the National Hockey League. He hoped some of Kyle's hockey magic would rub off on him.

Now, Cody swung his hips sideways and cut the blades of his skates deep into the ice for a sudden stop. The Elks' player defending against him tripped over himself and fell to the ice. Cody had a free lane to the net. Meanwhile, Kyle was hovering, wide open, just in front of the Elks' crease.

With his keen hockey sense, Cody made a split-second decision. He angled towards the net, his eyes boring into the goalie's. The goalie veered out to challenge him. Cody propelled himself forward, raising his stick to prepare for the shot. The goalie stood his ground, swivelling his padded body slightly to cut down on Cody's angle.

Then, at the last moment, just as the goalie's body tensed for the coming shot, Cody turned his shoulders and feathered a perfect pass to Kyle. The Elks' goalie, already committed to the faked shot, found his legs twisted in a knot. He sprawled to the ground and flung his glove hand uselessly back towards the open part of the net. At the same time, Kyle one-timed Cody's pass. Using his powerful wrists, he flicked his stick to lift the puck a few centimetres off the ice and sent it slicing to the net. As the black disk struck the mesh of the net, tenting it back, Cody lifted his arms in celebration, his heart soaring.

SHARKS 11, ELKS 3, the scoreboard read. Once again, the Transcona Sharks were routing their opponents. With Kyle Kelley at centre, there was no stopping them. The team was in a league of its own. And Cody was sure glad he was along for the ride. Playing organized hockey for the Transcona Sharks was turning out to be more fun this year than he had ever imagined.

"Way to go, buddy! Great pass," Kyle said to Cody as he clutched him close to his chest. "That one brings me up to nine goals."

Cody beamed. He and Winnipeg East scoring sensation Kyle Kelley were becoming best buddies. He was grateful for the day they were put on the same line.

By then all the Sharks' players on the ice had gathered around in a tight circle of turquoise and grey jerseys, congratulating Kyle and Cody with affectionate slaps on the shoulders. As the duo made their way to the bench, more cheers greeted them, this time from Coach Franklin and the rest of the players, a bunch that included, to Cody's delight, his long-time pals Ryan Miller and Ernie Gaines.

Seeing them now reminded Cody of this time last year, when Ryan, Ernie, and Cody, as well as their other friend Mitch Porter, had had to satisfy their craving for hockey by playing on the old outdoor rink next to the CN rail yards. Shivering in sub-zero cold, the boys usually had to shovel the snow themselves to clear the ice, and they used aluminum garbage cans as goal posts.

What a difference a year can make! The Transcona Community Club featured Sharks teams for boys and girls aged six to sixteen, but back then, indoor league hockey had been out of the question: Ryan was afraid of getting hurt, Ernie couldn't skate, Cody couldn't afford the equipment and registration costs, and Mitch was more interested in keeping stats than making them. Then Cody had impressed Coach Bartlett with his abilities and won a spot on the twelve-year-old Sharks' team through a program for kids whose parents couldn't afford to pay for league hockey. That year had turned out to be so much fun for Cody that this year he'd convinced his pals to try out for the thirteen-year-old Sharks' team. Ryan and Ernie had made the team. Mitch hadn't, but he'd become the team's official statistician and videographer. He was up in the stands right now, Cody noticed, training his camera on the face-off at centre ice.

It made a big difference to Cody to have his close friends with him on the team this year.

"Good job, boys," Coach Franklin offered, as Kyle and Cody took a seat on the Sharks' bench. A tall, solidly built man, Joe Franklin was the Sharks' coach, his first season in that role. He had a face that often looked sad, and huge, thick hands that he seemed unsure what to do with. Word had trickled down from some of the parents that he had once played International League hockey. "That was a smart set up, Cody, and a great shot, Kyle."

"Yeah, thanks," Kyle muttered. Cody knew Kyle wasn't too fond of Coach Franklin. Kyle complained that even though the coach knew his hockey, he didn't have enough of the killer instinct a good hockey coach needed, especially in thirteen-year-old league hockey, where bodychecking was allowed. Coach Franklin was big on fairness and clean play and giving everybody ice time. Fairness and clean play were all right, Cody thought, but Coach Franklin took his policy too far. Sometimes you had to play certain people to make sure you won the game.

Kyle took off his helmet, his blond locks tumbling out. He grabbed a water bottle and soaked his head, then squirted water into his mouth. He glanced up at the clock. "Three minutes left in the third period," he said, as the theme from the movie *Jaws* played over the intercom system. "Plenty of time for me to score my tenth goal."

Mitch had scampered down the stands to a spot just behind the bench and was zooming the camera in on Kyle's face. "That would be a record," Mitch pointed out admiringly.

Kyle tilted his head back, eyes closed, and swabbed his wet face with a towel. "Maybe in this league," he said, not even turning to look Mitch in the eyes. He was used to people talking to him while he went about his hockey business. "Last year, on my other team, I scored twelve goals in one game."

"Wow!" Cody exclaimed. He bit his lower lip and shook his head in amazement.

"That's like four hat tricks in one game," Mitch added. He scanned up and down Kyle's body with his camera.

"You got it," Kyle responded. He handled compliments like the star he was, Cody thought — like they were no big deal. As if they were simply a statement of the obvious.

"Next shift, I'll make sure to feed you a pass," Cody volunteered.

"Thanks, buddy," Kyle responded. "I'd appreciate that."

"Any time!" Cody blurted. "With you at centre, I'm having a great year. I've got seven goals already this season and …"

"Thirty-three assists!" Mitch put in. "Which makes you the number two scorer in the league. Next to Kyle, of course."

Cody leaned back against the hard bench and took a long look through the stands, packed to the rafters with spectators. He knew that most of the spectators were there to see Kyle Kelley, so that when they watched him one day on *Hockey Night in Canada* they could say they'd seen him play hockey when he was just a kid. Still, it was thrilling to play in front of such a big crowd. There was even a rumour that a National Hockey League scout would be showing up at a Sharks game soon, to take a close look at Kyle. Cody wondered if the scout was in the stands right now, and if he'd seen Cody make all those great passes to Kyle. Who knows? Cody thought. Maybe I can be in the NHL one day, just like Kyle. His spine tingled with the thought.

For a moment, too, Cody wished his dad were here to watch him play, especially now that he was on a line with Kyle and scoring so many points. Last Christmas, when Cody had travelled with his little sister Letisha (everybody called her Tish) to Kamloops, British Columbia to visit his dad, his dad had mentioned that maybe the following Christmas he might return the favour and visit them. Cody hoped that was true. Divorce or no divorce, his dad should have been able to watch him play a few games.

The referee's whistle blew suddenly and jolted Cody from his reverie. He and Kyle were due on the ice for the next shift. He retied his skate laces tighter around his ankles, as he did before every shift, as a kind of superstition, and stood up to climb out onto the ice. Kyle propped himself up on his stick right behind him, ready to follow.

But Coach Franklin held his bulky arms out over the bench door, like a patrol holding back pedestrians from a crosswalk. "Boys, you've had a great game," he said. "I think it's time to give some of the other players a chance, too. Ryan, why don't you take the left wing, and Sean, you can play centre."

In an instant Ryan and Sean hopped over the bench and onto the ice, wide smiles splitting their faces. Mitch followed the new players onto the ice with his camera. Meanwhile, Cody's jaw dropped. He wanted a chance to feed Kyle his tenth goal of the night.

Kyle speared his stick behind the bench and kicked the coach's duffel bag full of extra equipment. "This sucks!" he spat out. "Totally sucks!"

"Yeah!" Cody echoed his linemate. He was happy for his friend Ryan, he supposed, but he really wanted to get back out there with Kyle to score even more goals. It didn't make any sense to stop the pair now when they were as hot as they were. Coach Franklin didn't know what he was doing.

"Please, boys, try to understand," Coach Franklin said. His hands were tucked awkwardly into his armpits. "We're way ahead. It's only fair to give some of the other boys some ice time."

"Give them ice time in practice," Kyle barked. "This is a real game. I'm going for a record, you know. Ten goals in one game." He looked directly into Coach Franklin's eyes, challenging him. "That's never been done on this team before."

"What difference does it make, nine goals, ten goals? You've had plenty of ice time. Now it's time to give somebody else a chance."

"Those guys can't even play hockey," Kyle murmured, his chin nodding derisively towards the ice. At that moment, Ryan was bodychecked against the boards and had the puck stolen from him by an Elks' forward, as if confirming Kyle's evaluation. "They're wimps."

Coach Franklin's face reddened with anger. He clasped his hands as if to keep them from striking out. "I can't accept comments like that on this team," he said. "And this is a team, you might want to remember. A team made up of twenty players, nineteen of whom are not named Kyle Kelley but are just as important as any other player on this team." He took a deep breath. "I think it would be best if you spent the rest of the game in the dressing room."

"Have it your way," Kyle commented disgustedly. He took off his helmet and shoved it under his arm. At the same time, the Elks moved in to score an easy goal and the goal buzzer went off. Kyle shook his head. "You just might lose this game yet, Coach," he jabbed, glancing up at the scoreboard as the number beside the ELKS changed to a 4. "Good luck."

Cody felt the adrenaline that had been pumping through his body suddenly drain away. His body went limp and his forehead began to sweat. This isn't the way it's supposed to be, he thought. Kyle was the star on this team, he was the reason the arena was filled, he was the one all eyes were following. You couldn't bench him. No, if you were a smart coach, you put him on the ice and let him do his magic. That's just the way it was. Coach Franklin was an idiot not to see that. He could ruin the whole season like this, for Kyle, for Cody, and for the whole team, for that matter.

In his frustration, Cody slumped down on the bench and kicked his skates out in front of him, making a loud banging sound against the wooden boards.

"Do you want to join your linemate?" Coach Franklin asked suddenly, anger lacing his words. Cody was startled. He didn't think the coach had noticed him.

Kyle stopped in his tracks. He glanced back at Cody. Sweat glistened on Kyle's face and his eyes burned with defiance. He was asking Cody to support him, to show Coach Franklin that he couldn't get away with what he was doing, that he was being unfair to Kyle.

Cody didn't know what to do. It wasn't like him to stand up to a coach, but he wanted to show his loyalty to Kyle. It was Kyle who had helped make Cody a star on the Transcona Sharks. It was Kyle who would lead Cody to the Winnipeg East all-star team. If he stuck by him now, their friendship would be sealed.

Not knowing exactly what he was doing or why, trying his best to hide the little tremors of fear and tension that were pulsing through his body, Cody stood up and walked behind Kyle, not even looking back at Coach Franklin.

"Hold on," he said. "I'm coming too."

# 2

# The Dating Game

"Mom, can we stop at the mall?" Cody asked. "I need to look for some new elbow pads. My old ones are worn out."

Cody's mom had come by the arena with Tish to pick up Cody. Last year, his mom and sister had been able to attend most of his games, at least the ones in Transcona, but this year Tish was too busy with her own activities, like choir practice and karate lessons. Now, Cody was worried about the consequences of his recent actions after the game against the Elks. He was hoping that a new piece of hockey equipment might get his mind off his problems.

"Can't this wait for some other time?" Cody's mom asked, keeping her eyes on the road. The car windows were still partly fogged. Outside, colourful Christmas lights lit up the trees on the boulevard as night enveloped the sky like a black blanket. "I'm kind of in a hurry."

"They only cost about fifteen dollars, Mom," Cody put in. "I've saved up the money myself so you don't have to pay, if that's what you're worried about."

"It's not that," his mom said.

"Well, what is it then?" Cody asked. With the palm of his hand, he wiped the moisture off his side of the window.

"Like I said, I'm in a hurry," his mom replied, fumbling to light a cigarette with the lighter on the dashboard. She had been trying to quit off and on for over a year.

"A hurry?" Cody's eyebrows furrowed. "What's the occasion? I mean, it's Thursday night. What are you going to do except get home, put on your bathrobe and slippers, pop a huge bowl of popcorn, and watch *ER* with Tish?"

"Nothing's up. I just have something to do tonight." Cody sensed a nervous catch in his mom's voice. He wondered if something was bothering her. Maybe his dad had called and upset her. That happened sometimes since the divorce, usually when they talked about money. Those times were rough on his mom, he knew.

"Mom, we don't have to go to the mall tonight," he said. He looked out the window at the passing traffic. Exhaust fumes filled the air. Snowbanks loomed like miniature mountains at the side of the road. "I'll go myself tomorrow after school."

"Thanks," his mom said. She seemed to relax. Cody couldn't help wondering again what was bothering her. Maybe she was having trouble at work. It seemed to Cody that there was always talk of layoffs at the railway where she worked in the welding shop.

"Don't mention it, Mom," Cody put in.

Just then, eight-year-old Tish poked her head into the space between the two front seats. "Could you guys keep it down up there, please?" she requested. "I'm trying to listen to the radio." She leaned forward and turned the volume knob louder. "The *Dr. Muldoon Show* is about to start again."

"Aren't you sick of that program yet?" Cody whined. The *Dr. Muldoon Show* featured people who called a psychologist for advice regarding family problems. "It's always the same thing: 'take control of your life,' 'learn to face reality,' 'stick by your decisions,' and all that kind of stuff. It gets tiring after a while."

Cody's mom cut in. "Cody, if Tish likes the program, she can listen to it." She glanced into the rearview mirror to spot Tish. "That is, if she sits back and tightens her seat belt."

Tish squirmed back into her seat. Then she put her index finger to her lips and mouthed a big "Please!" one more time. Cody and his mom chuckled. "OK," Cody said. "We'll be quiet."

The caller on the *Dr. Muldoon Show* was prattling on and on about a boyfriend she couldn't trust. Cody tried to tune out the program. I've got my own problems, he thought, I don't have to listen to other people's, too. He closed his eyes and settled back into his seat. In his mind he replayed the goals he and Kyle had scored that night. Soon he found himself forgetting his recent act of defiance and being caught up once again in the excitement of the game.

If he just blanked Coach Franklin from his mind, Cody saw this year on the Sharks as a dream season.

At the commercial break, Cody's mom cleared her throat as if she had something to say. She turned to glance at Cody. "Aren't you going to ask what I have to do tonight?" she inquired.

Cody popped his eyes open, distracted from his hockey thoughts. Again, he sensed a kind of tension in his mom's voice.

"I guess so," he said. "I just wanted to give you some space, that's all. I figured you had a rough day or something."

His mom's face warmed. "Thanks," she said. "But no, I haven't had a rough day." A tiny smile curled her lips. "In fact, it's been rather pleasant."

"What do you mean?" Cody asked.

"Well, something which I think is very nice happened to me today." She lowered her eyes. "I just hope you agree."

Cody was lost. His mom didn't usually beat around the bush like this. Something was up, and he wanted to find out exactly what, as quickly as possible.

Just then, the *Dr. Muldoon Show* started up again, and Tish, index finger back at her lips, called for absolute silence.

"Out with it, Mom!" Cody demanded, in as much of a whisper as he could manage.

"Well, you know I've been staying home with you and Tish pretty much every night since your dad left us almost two years ago." Cody's mom, too, was whispering.

"Yeah, I guess so," Cody agreed. "But you do go to bingo with Grams every Saturday night."

"I know."

"What is it? Do you want to go out with Sheila tonight?" Sheila was his mom's best friend. She was divorced, too. "That's not a problem. I can take care of Tish."

"Thanks," his mom offered. Her voice seemed to lose some of its nervous edge. "I do want to go out tonight." She looked directly into Cody's eyes, waiting a few beats before resuming. "I've been asked out." She waited a few more beats, then added, "On a date. Is that OK? Because if it's not …"

Cody was shocked. The last thing he expected from his mom right now was that she'd ask to go out on a date. Now that I'm thirteen years old, aren't *I* the one who's supposed to be asking *her* if *I* can go out on dates and stuff? he thought. But then he realized the idea made sense. Besides working at the CN shops all day, his mom was always stuck in the house with Tish and him and had little social life. Meanwhile, his dad was living in Kamloops with Della and her two kids. Not that there was anything wrong with Della, because Cody had sure enjoyed his time with her and his dad in Kamloops last Christmas. But he realized now that his mom might want someone like Della in her life, too. She may be our mom, but she's also human, he thought. And since Tish and I are her family, we have to support her.

"It's OK," Cody said finally.

"It's OK?" his mom asked again, obviously surprised at Cody's quick approval of her request.

Cody nodded his head. "Yeah, it's OK, Mom." He looked squarely at her. "I mean, I think I understand, at least a little bit. Ernie's mom is divorced, and she dates. I think I can handle it."

Cody's mom broke into a laugh that sounded almost like a cry. She took one hand off the steering wheel and patted Cody's head. "You're some kid, you know that?" she said. "I'm glad you're mine."

"Thanks," Cody said. He felt his throat go dry.

Tish cut in suddenly. "Guys, you're getting too loud again," she complained, reaching forward to turn up the volume. "I can't even hear what Dr. Muldoon's saying."

Cody turned to look at his little sister. "Oh, sorry," he said mockingly. "It's just that mom was telling me that she's going out on a date tonight and —"

"A date!" Tish squealed. She thrust her hand forward quickly to turn off the radio. "What are you talking about?"

Cody smiled wryly. "But what about Dr. Muldoon?"

"Dr. Muldoon can wait," Tish cried. Her blond braids jiggled. She turned to her mom. "It's not true, Mom, is it, you're not going on a date, are you?"

"Actually, Tish, I think I am," her mother answered, her voice tender, careful. One of her eyes was on the road, the other looking at Tish in the rearview mirror.

"Mom!" Tish squawked.

Tish had told Cody that her prayers each night included a plea that one day their mom and dad would get back together again.

"Tish, it should be fine," he tried to explain now. "Adults date. It happens all the time. Look at Dad."

"But she's our mom!" Tish cried out. Tears were streaming down her cheeks. "It's not right. It just isn't right. What if Dad wants to come back, what then?"

"Tish, that's not going to happen, at least not the way you're hoping," their mom said. "You know that. Your dad and I have talked about this with you so many times. Please try to understand."

"I can't!"

Tish and Cody's mom shook her head and leaned back far into the car seat.

"Tish, Mom needs to have a life of her own," Cody put in. "If you were a little older, you could understand that. That's just the way it is."

"No, no, no!" Tish protested.

"Tish, you're not being reasonable," Cody added. His mom had been quiet a few seconds now and he felt he had to stick up for her. "It's only a date."

Tish wiped the tears from her face, trying to compose herself. "Why, Mom?"

"I think I'm ready again to enjoy the company of a man, that's all," her mom replied. She twisted her hand to the back and found Tish's, squeezing it. "I can understand how you're feeling, honey, but, believe me, you don't have to be worried. My dating doesn't change anything with us. Nothing."

Tish sniffled. She grabbed a tissue from the box on the ledge at the back of the car and blew her nose. "Do we know him?" Tish asked. "The man you're going out on a date with?"

"As a matter of fact, you do," Cody's mom replied. "And I think you'll be pleased with my choice."

Suddenly, Cody's interest was heightened. He was OK with his mom dating, but now that it was someone he knew, he wondered how he'd react. He felt his heart racing. "Who is it, Mom? Tell us!" he demanded.

They had arrived at the house and their mom put the car into park. Then she turned to her kids. "It's Joe Franklin," she said. "He asked me out after your last game, Cody."

# 3

## Practice Doesn't Always Make Perfect

Y ou don't look so good," Ryan commented to Cody as they dressed for practice. "Are you sick or something?"

"No, I'm just having an off day," Cody responded, keeping his eyes averted from his friend's. He halfheartedly laced up his skates.

"Well, you look sick to me, pal," Ryan continued. "If I were you, I think I'd sit this practice out."

In fact, Cody *did* feel sick, but not in the high temperature and aching head kind of way. Ever since his mom had told him three days ago that she was going on a date with Coach Franklin, he wasn't so sure that he wanted to keep playing for the Transcona Sharks. He had never really disliked Coach Franklin as a person before, but since then he thought that maybe he did. In fact, he maybe even hated him. He no longer felt so bad about having defied the coach, either. As for his mom, he had made it perfectly clear to her at the time that he hoped she would break her date with Coach Franklin, but she had insisted that it wouldn't have been polite. Couldn't she have chosen someone else, Cody thought now, someone other than his hockey coach, to date? He felt betrayed. Even though he hadn't asked her about it, he hoped that they'd gone out on their date and had a terrible time. He hoped that now the whole business was over and done with.

Cody looked around the dressing room for Kyle. He was nowhere to be seen. Maybe he decided to quit the team after Coach Franklin didn't let him play the final minutes of the last game, Cody thought. Kyle would have the guts to do that. Teams around the league would be lined up to have him sign with them.

Cody also wondered whether Coach Franklin would make any mention of him hitting the dressing room early last game. He'd better not, Cody thought, or I'll mention him going out with my mom. How would he like that?

In a few minutes the Sharks took the ice for their practice, and Cody reluctantly joined them. Lord Strathcona Arena was empty now, except for the caretaker sweeping up discarded coffee and soda cups and potato chip bags from between the stands, and the Zamboni driver polishing up the last stretch of ice. The sound of pucks ricocheting against the boards or rattling the goal posts echoed loudly. A muggy fog pressed down against the ice surface. Cody felt a chill run down his spine, and he had to take a few deep breaths to shake it off. He gripped his stick tighter in his hands and took some long, loping strides on his skates. It felt good to glide across the ice again. Maybe it was odd, he thought, but playing hockey — or sometimes just thinking about playing hockey — seemed to be the one way he could get his mind off his problems.

Coach Franklin blew his whistle to sound the beginning of practice. "Come on in, guys. It's time to get the show on the road."

Cody followed Ryan and Ernie as the Sharks gathered around their coach at centre ice. Since the beginning of the season, the three of them had hung around together at practices, and they even did their own practising — with Mitch in tow — on the outdoor rink. Of course, lately Cody had been spending some time with Kyle, too, although for the most part, Kyle kept to himself during practices. Cody wondered if that would change now that the two boys seemed to be growing closer.

Coach Franklin loomed like a bear above the boys as he discussed the good and bad points of the team's recent performance against the Elks. He was certainly a big man, Cody had to admit to himself. No question about it, Coach Franklin looked like he could have played International League hockey. He could have been the team bully. That's the way he was built.

"I want you guys to separate into pairs and work on your passing," Coach Franklin commanded. "Start by making short passes to each other and then open up the space between you."

He blew his whistle again to signal the start of the drill. Cody was glad the coach hadn't pulled him aside for a personal lecture or anything. He supposed Coach Franklin was willing to forget last game's episode.

"Are we partners?" Ryan asked Cody.

Cody looked around once more for Kyle, but still the Sharks' star player had not shown up. "Sure," he replied.

Ryan and Cody started passing to each other, first short, tight passes, then longer trajectories. They were familiar with each other's style, and it was easy to execute the drill. How many nights have we spent together on the outdoor rink doing much the same thing? Cody thought. Now all that hard work was paying off.

"That was some game the other night," Ryan began. "We really walloped those Elks!"

"You can say that again," Cody concurred. "Kyle scored nine goals. Nine goals! Can you believe it?"

"I know," Ryan said. "He was really something." Ryan returned a pass to Cody and the puck landed firmly on his friend's stick. "Did you see the breakaway I made?" Ryan continued. "It was in the last minute, and I deked the defence-man. I was in alone against the goalie." Ryan smiled. He was what coaches called a "finesse" player. He had some good moves, but he liked to keep his distance from the rough stuff. "My shot was wide, but what a thrill! I'm sure glad Coach Franklin let me play."

"I missed that," Cody admitted. Ryan's breakaway must have happened while Cody was in the dressing room with Kyle after their run-in with Coach Franklin — and after the game had already been won by Kyle and Cody's scoring bonanza. "But did you see that setup I made for Kyle's last goal, where I faked the shot and totally fooled the goalie? Wasn't that awesome?"

"Yeah, it was," Ryan said.

"I scored two goals and four assists — that's six points," Cody added. "That makes me number two in the league. After Kyle." Cody grinned. He was suddenly feeling better. "I think I might even make the all-star team this year."

"I know," Ryan said. "Why don't we go over to Mitch's house tonight to watch the game? He told me he has my breakaway on tape. That way you can see it."

"Sounds fine with me," Cody offered. "I'm not doing anything tonight." He glanced suddenly at Coach Franklin and stiffened with bitterness. "Unless I have to take care of my sister because my mom's going out."

"What?" Ryan asked, not quite understanding what Cody was saying.

"Nothing," Cody replied. "Nothing."

\*\*\*

As the drill came to an end, from the corner of his eye Cody noticed Kyle sauntering onto the ice. He turned to look, as Kyle adjusted his helmet and sped towards Coach Franklin.

"Sorry, Coach, I got caught up with something," Kyle announced. "Hope that's not a problem."

Coach Franklin eyed Kyle a few seconds and then pursed his lips, like he was considering what to do about Kyle being late. Finally, he spoke. "It's OK," he said, "this time. But being late for practice without a valid excuse is not something I want to see my players get into the habit of doing."

"I'll try not to let it happen again," Kyle retorted.

"I hope so," Coach Franklin said.

The practice continued, with Coach Franklin letting the boys play a scrimmage game. Soon Cody was enjoying once again playing on a line with someone as talented as Kyle. Kyle flew up and down the ice as if nothing could stop him, and usually nothing did. In no time Kyle and Cody had racked up several goals, and Cody noticed that the arena, empty only a few minutes ago, was slowly filling with people who wanted to get a glimpse of Kyle Kelley at work. There were parents, other kids, other coaches, the caretaker and the Zamboni driver, and even the Transcona Sharks hockey club manager, Lou Phelps, who was in charge of the whole league hockey operation at Lord Strathcona Arena.

Hockey fans were attracted to Kyle like bees to honey, Cody thought.

At one point during the scrimmage Kyle and Cody were on a breakaway against Ryan and Sean, with Ernie in net. Cody, who held the puck, was excited at the prospect of trying to outplay his pals, who knew all his best moves. That would be quite a challenge. Skating down the ice, he moved in towards Ryan, readying himself to try to slip the puck between his friend's skates, then pick up the loose puck and charge the net or pass to Kyle. He kept his eyes on Ryan and made sure not to move his shoulders in a way that would give away his plan.

Suddenly, out of nowhere, Kyle appeared between Cody and Ryan, and barrelled into Ryan like a steam engine, sending him flying to the ice. Ryan lay sprawled at the blue line, unmoving. Cody froze, looking dumbly from his fallen friend to the free lane to the net that had been opened in front of him by Kyle's bold bodycheck. Meanwhile, Ernie charged out of the net to take a swipe at Kyle, in retaliation for the hit his friend had taken.

A whistle blew, and Coach Franklin came racing onto the ice. First he separated Ernie and Kyle, throwing them apart with one quick push of his massive arms, and then he rushed to Ryan's side. Cody followed him.

"Are you all right?" the coach asked Ryan. The coach's face was white as the ice. His voice crackled with anxiety.

Ryan stirred and then lifted his upper body off the ice. "Yeah, I'll be OK," he said. He rubbed his shoulders and then stood up. He nodded his head. "I'm OK. I am."

"For sure?" Cody asked, concerned. He knew Ryan didn't take too well to being hit.

"For sure," Ryan said. "It wasn't so bad, except that I didn't see the check coming." He glanced around for some evidence of who had just steamrolled him.

Kyle skated to the group huddled around Ryan. "Sorry," he said. "I was just going to the net. You know how it is."

"That was a cheap shot," Coach Franklin reprimanded Kyle. His voice was stern. "You could have seriously hurt Ryan."

"Sorry," Kyle said. "These things happen."

"Well, they shouldn't," Coach Franklin said. "Not in a practice, and not even in a game. Safety should be your number one consideration. You kids are here to have fun and maybe learn a little something about what it takes to build a winning team, not to hurt one another." He turned to Ryan and reached out to pat him on the shoulder. "You're sure you're OK?"

"Yes, Coach," Ryan responded, "I'm fine."

"Just to ease my mind, at least," the coach said, "I think you should go over to the trainer's office." He looked around at the team. "Who's going to volunteer to help Ryan to the trainer's office?"

Ernie sprang out of the crowd. "I will," he said. He grabbed his friend under the shoulders and helped him off the ice.

Kyle turned to Coach Franklin. "Being physical's just part of the game," he said. "You can't make the NHL unless you're willing to hit and be hit."

Coach Franklin rolled his eyes. "Let's not worry too much about the NHL," he said. His eyes took on a grim cast again, as if what he was about to say was the most important thing he could tell these boys. "You have no idea how badly you could hurt someone out on the ice without even meaning to," he added, rubbing his eyes and letting out a sigh. He seemed about to say more, then changed his mind. "Practice is over. Hit the showers, boys!"

*** 

"What's Coach Franklin's problem, anyhow?" Kyle asked Cody as the two of them headed off the ice.

"What do you mean?" Cody asked.

"He's so against hitting, it's ridiculous," Kyle said. "He shouldn't be a hockey coach if he doesn't like hitting. Ask anybody who knows anything about hockey — it's a violent sport."

"I guess so," Cody offered.

"I'll tell you this much," Kyle continued. "The NHL isn't interested in wimps. My dad tells me that all the time."

That made sense to Cody. If you wanted to play professional hockey, you had to be tough, and you had to be willing to play rough. Coach Franklin wasn't doing a good job of preparing the boys for professional hockey.

"I don't know," Kyle went on. "Maybe when he was a player Coach Franklin was hit by some goon and got injured. Maybe that explains his wimpy attitude."

"Maybe," Cody agreed, although it was difficult to picture someone knocking Coach Franklin off his feet.

As the boys proceeded down the cement corridor leading to the dressing room, they were stopped by two girls who had been sitting in the stands. Cody recognized them from school but he couldn't remember their names. He followed Kyle as he stepped closer to them.

"Great practice, guys. You really looked good out there," one of the girls said.

"Thanks," Kyle responded. He looked at the two girls carefully. "You're Lanya and you're Kirsten, right? We met at the last game."

"That's right," the girl named Lanya said. "We come to most of the games."

"Our next home game's against the St. Vital Marauders," Kyle mentioned. "Maybe we'll see you there." Kyle was so smooth and confident, Cody thought. He admired that.

"For sure," Lanya said. "I never miss a Sharks' game."

"All right, then," Kyle said.

"Well, what are you guys doing tonight?" Kirsten asked. "I mean, if you're not busy, maybe you could meet us at the mall. We're going there after supper."

"Sounds good to me," Kyle said. "What do you say, buddy?" He turned to Cody.

Cody was caught up in the excitement of the moment. He never got much attention from girls at school and now all of a sudden he was going to meet some at the mall. This was neat. He kind of liked being a hockey hero.

"Sure," he said.

"So we'll meet at the food court at about seven-thirty," Kyle said to the girls and to Cody.

"Yeah," the girls said. "It's a date."

"Yeah," Cody chimed in. "I'll be there."

Suddenly, Cody remembered that he'd promised Ryan he'd meet him at Mitch's house to watch the videotape of the game against the Elks. But he couldn't go back on his plans with Kyle. Not now that they were becoming good friends. I'll call tonight to make sure Ryan is OK and explain why I can't make it, he figured. The boys will understand, Cody thought.

They're my friends.

# 4

# A Date at the Mall

"Take a look at this!" Kyle called out to Cody from deep inside the All-Pro Sporting Goods Store. He held up a fancy black-handled hockey stick made from burnished wood. "Imagine the goals I could score with this!"

The two boys were at the mall killing time before they were to meet with Lanya and Kirsten. They drifted from store to store, picking out interesting items and making funny comments about them.

"How about this?" Cody responded. He tried on a candy-apple-red helmet that looked like it could belong to an astronaut. "I could get smacked over the head and I wouldn't feel a thing."

"You think so, hey?" Kyle moved towards Cody. Playfully, he tapped Cody on the helmet with the hockey stick. The stick made a loud clang that echoed through the store, but Cody was unhurt.

"Told you," Cody said, "my head's fine." Then he took off the helmet and faked lolling his head on his shoulders and falling to the ground as if knocked out. Kyle laughed uproariously.

"You're cool, Cody," Kyle said. "It's good to have someone like you on the Sharks. A lot of the other guys on the team … I don't know, they seem like twerps."

Cody felt uncomfortable calling the guys on the Sharks twerps, especially since several of them were his good friends, but he didn't want to make too big a deal of it right now with Kyle. "Some of them are all right," he said.

"Well, you know, my dad always says that this world's full of winners and losers, and you have to decide which bunch you want to belong to. Personally, I want to be a winner. Like my dad. He was the number one real estate agent in Winnipeg two months ago."

"Really?" Cody asked.

"You bet," Kyle announced proudly. "He's promised to be my agent when I sign with an NHL club. He's a real winner."

Cody was silent for a moment. He was wondering whether his own dad was a winner or a loser. He'd like to think his dad was a winner, but he wasn't sure what to go on. His dad did all right when it came to making money, especially since he got a new job at a particle board plant in Kamloops, but he still complained that there wasn't enough for this or for that. Then there was the divorce. In that case, Cody wasn't sure who was the winner and who was the loser. As far as he was concerned, his whole family had lost, in a way, because they lost something that they thought they would have forever.

"I'm going to make sure I'm always a winner," Kyle went on. Cody couldn't help but believe his new friend. There was something about him — the way he looked, the way his body moved — that indicated he was made for great things. Cody wished he was like that, too. Something inside him told him that he could be, if he just worked at it, if he just stuck by Kyle.

"At least on the Sharks we'll be winners," Cody said. "I don't think there's a team in the Winnipeg East division that can beat us."

"Not in all of Winnipeg," Kyle said. "That's as long as Coach Franklin doesn't ruin things for us. Now there's a loser for you."

"What do you mean?"

"Like I always say, Coach Franklin just doesn't have the killer instinct you need to win hockey games. He's a wimp."

"I'm not too keen on him either," Cody said, thinking not only of Coach Franklin's limitations as a coach, but also of the fact that he had gone out with Cody's mom. "But we haven't lost a game yet."

"That's not the point. We could be even better. Coach Franklin is keeping the Sharks back by playing all those other guys who don't know the first thing about hockey," Kyle added. "Mr. Phelps, the hockey manager, is a good friend of my dad's, and even he's not happy with Coach Franklin. Mr. Phelps says he'll can him if he has to, if it ever comes down to making the difference between winning and losing."

"Really?" Cody had no idea people other than himself and his teammates cared so much about whether the Transcona Sharks won or lost their hockey games.

The store manager approached the boys, with a stern look on his face.

"What's going on back here, boys? May I help you with something?"

Cody realized he was still holding the fancy red helmet in his hands, so he quickly put it back on the shelf. "No, sir, we were just looking," he said.

The store manager leaned over huffily and rearranged the helmet so that it fit in with the rest of the helmets on display the way it was supposed to.

"Actually, I'm kind of interested in this stick," Kyle said. He winked at Cody, who had no idea what his friend was up to. "Could you tell me a little more about it?"

"Well, son, this is one of our very own All-Pro line of sticks." He leaned over to take hold of the stick, but Kyle had gripped it tightly and was taking some practice shots in the air. "It's a little pricey, of course, but well worth the money."

Kyle looked directly at the store manager. "I'm on the Transcona Sharks and I use a Sher-Wood stick now, but I sure wouldn't mind trying this model."

"Of course," the store manager exclaimed, "you're Kyle Kelley! I thought I recognized you when you entered the store, but I wasn't sure." He smiled from ear to ear and shook his head. "How could I have missed you? I saw you playing just the other night over at Lord Strathcona Arena. That was some show you put on!"

"Nine goals," Kyle pointed out.

"Right, right, you were fantastic. You know, Lou Phelps says he's never seen a player like you come through this league. Never. You're destined for the NHL, boy! Gonna make Transcona famous!"

"I plan on it," Kyle said. He handed the hockey stick to the store manager. The manager twirled it in his hands a few times. Then he leaned his chin on its handle, thinking.

"You know, I'm one of the sponsors of the Sharks," he mentioned. "I've got a proposition for you. Let me take a picture of you with this stick and maybe some other All-Pro equipment, wearing your Transcona Sharks' jersey, of course, and I'll let you have this stick: free, gratis, a gift from me to you. How does that sound?"

Kyle didn't hesitate a second. "Sure," he said, grinning. He threw a discreet thumbs up Cody's way. "When do you want me to come down for the picture?"

"Leave your number with me and I'll give you a call when I have a photographer booked." The manager glanced at the front wall of the store. "I'll hang the picture right over there where all my customers can see it and know that All-Pro equipment makes winners."

"Sounds fine with me," Kyle nodded his head. "But can I have the stick now? I'd love to use it next game." He looked across at Cody. "And how about some elbow pads for my friend. He's Cody Powell, the left-winger on my line. He feeds me all those passes I turn into goals."

The store manager laughed softly. "You drive a hard bargain, son. I admire that. Sure, take the stick today and a pair of elbow pads for your friend. Maybe you guys will remember me when you're famous."

"We sure will," Kyle said. "Thanks."

The second the boys had walked far enough away from the All-Pro store to be sure the store manager could no longer see them, they hooted and hollered and high-fived each other.

"That was amazing!" Cody panted. "I can't believe it."

"I had that guy eating out of the palm of my hand." Kyle was beaming with pride. "I told you it pays to be a winner in this world."

"You're right!" Cody reached into his bag and pulled out his loot. "New elbow pads, and I didn't spend a dime!"

"Stick with me, buddy, and there'll be more where this came from."

"I will!" Cody announced.

Kyle looked suddenly at his watch. "Oops! We're late for our date," he said. "Follow me to the food court."

Cody might as well have been walking on air. This is too good to be true, he thought. The excitement of the moment, the sheer thrill of hanging around with Kyle, gripped him, but he also felt a strange nervousness, similar to when he walked onto a scary new ride at the Red River Exhibition. This was fun, but it was somehow dangerous, too. It felt like anything could happen.

The boys approached the food court and scanned the tables for Lanya and Kirsten.

"Guys, we're over here!" Lanya's voice travelled across the mall.

Kyle spun his head around quickly. "The girls are at the arcade," he reported. He hurried away from the food court towards the rear of the mall.

But Cody didn't turn to follow. His eyes were focussed on a table right in the middle of the food court. His mom was sitting there with a cup of coffee in front of her, and seated across from her was a man: Coach Franklin.

I should have known this day was too good to be true, Cody thought.

Obviously, his mom was continuing to see Coach Franklin even though Cody had asked her not to.

Once again, Cody felt let down. Somehow or another, his mom or his dad always ruined things for him. And what bothered Cody most was that they did so knowing full well what they were doing. It just made no sense to him. No sense at all.

His eyes burned and he felt a sob welling up inside him. But he held it back. He wasn't going to let his mom ruin this day or this hockey season for him. He was going to fight back. He was going to be a winner, not a loser.

"Hold on, Kyle," he called out after his friend. "I'm right behind you."

***

When he met up with Kyle and the girls, Cody tried to be loose and have fun, but he just couldn't. Lanya, especially, seemed to like him and wanted to make conversation, but Cody just walked alongside her dumbly, like a dog. He would've liked to talk to her, to have fun with her, but his mind was someplace else, someplace back in the food court.

When he got home that night, he thought to himself, he would tell his mother that enough was enough! She had better not go on any more dates with Coach Franklin.

# 5

# The Sharks Bare Their Teeth

Come on, guys, hustle out there!" Mitch called out to Cody and the other Sharks' players on the ice, his camera glued to the action. "We need a goal!"

The Sharks were playing an exhibition match away from home, against the North End Raiders, and they found themselves in the unusual position of trailing by two goals well into the final period. Not only were the Raiders a scrappy, tough team that chipped away at opponents, they also had two speedy forwards — Lone Eagle McKay and Ramon Rebolo — who zipped easily around the Sharks' defence.

It certainly didn't help the Sharks' cause that, this being an exhibition game, Coach Franklin was giving extra ice time to the second and third liners.

Cody wasn't going to let any of that stop him from doing his best to win this game. He was determined to prove himself a winner, even if Coach Franklin only gave him a minute or two at a time to do so. And even if his mom set up obstacles along the way. The night after he'd seen his mom at the mall with Coach Franklin, Cody had spoken to her about how little he liked the idea of her going out with Coach Franklin. Her response had been that she'd make sure their dating would not get in the way of Cody's hockey. How could that be possible?

Cody kept thinking. My mom's dating my hockey coach — it's just not right.

Cody dug his skates into the ice and pushed himself forward, towards the puck. The Raiders' Lone Eagle McKay was bringing it up, waiting for his teammates to set themselves up for the drive to the net. Cody tried to thwart his plans. After outmuscling one defender, he crossed an open stretch of ice and approached Lone Eagle. Leaning his body forward, Cody poke-checked his opponent. In an instant, he could feel the puck's weight against the blade of his stick.

At the same time, Kyle sped down centre ice, his turquoise and grey uniform lighting up the rink. "I'm open!" he cried to Cody. "Wide open."

Cody felt Lone Eagle's breath against his face as the two boys struggled for control of the puck. Lone Eagle tried shoving Cody away, but Cody persisted, like a dog at a bone, throwing his weight at his adversary as he let out a loud grunt. Finally, Lone Eagle momentarily lost his footing, just long enough for Cody to squeeze the puck away and send a quick pass over to Kyle.

The thrill of making the play rushed through Cody's body like a roller coaster.

Kyle picked up the puck and veered towards the net. Two Raiders' defenders hung onto his hips but he threw them off like a wild bronco bucking off a rider. He hunkered down and flicked a wrist shot. The goalie moved to his right, but the puck zoomed over his left shoulder and into the net. A goal! The Sharks' bench cheered, and the scoreboard showed RAIDERS 3, SHARKS 2.

"Way to go, buddy!" Kyle congratulated Cody at centre ice, as they prepared for the face-off. "Great pass, once again!"

As several players clapped Cody on the back, his sense of exhilaration rose to a new level. He felt his body was now fine-tuned for one thing and one thing only — making a play to score another goal. The Raiders might be tough, but we can be tougher, he thought.

This is the way the great goal scorers — Gretzky, Selanne, Lindros — must feel when they hit the ice, Cody thought. He relished the feeling.

There was a tap on his shoulder. Cody turned to see Sean Halton standing behind him.

"Coach says it's our shift," Sean said.

"What?" Cody turned to the bench and saw Coach Franklin waving his big hands in a windmill motion, signalling for Cody, Kyle, and Tyler Wasniak, who was playing right wing, to leave the ice.

"You've got to be kidding!" Cody protested. He spat out the words.

Sean shrugged his shoulders. "Sorry, Cody, but those are Coach's orders." Sean skated into place for the face-off, as the referee looked on impatiently. "Who knows, we might even score a goal and tie this one up."

"Fat chance," Cody found himself saying. They were harsh words, he knew, but he was really riled now, and he didn't care who knew it. Taking Kyle and him off the ice was just plain stupid. He felt like a balloon that had been suddenly deflated.

At the bench Cody flung his helmet off and slumped against the hard wood of the seat. Kyle followed him, disgust misshaping his face. Coach Franklin ignored them, keeping his eyes on the boys on the ice.

Just then Mr. Phelps, the hockey manager, came stomping down from the viewing gallery upstairs. He was wearing a blue pinstriped suit with a big, gold-plated name tag on his lapel. He moved in right next to Coach Franklin.

"What's going on out there tonight, Coach?" he demanded. His breath made a cloud of fog in the cold arena air.

"We're losing, and all I can see is our star player spending half the time on the bench."

Kyle and Cody exchanged I-told-you-so expressions.

"We do have to make an effort to let the entire team play," Coach Franklin said evenly. "Especially since this isn't a game that has any bearing on the standings." He was standing firm, but Cody noticed his face flushing.

"Exhibition or not, I recommend you make an effort to win this game," Mr. Phelps instructed. "There are four hockey convenors from Ontario and Quebec up there in the viewing gallery with me deciding whether to invite us or the North End Raiders to the All-Canadian Hockey Tournament this spring in Toronto, and I want to make sure they don't leave here without having made the right decision. Get it?"

"A trip to Toronto!" some of the players on the bench exclaimed in unison. "All right! We have to win this one."

Cody and Kyle swapped animated looks.

But Coach Franklin persisted. "Mr. Phelps," he said, "let's not discuss this in front of the players. After the game would be a more appropriate time."

"That might be too late," Mr. Phelps responded. "Just make sure we win tonight." He stormed away, his suit jacket flapping untidily, his heels clicking loudly against the cement steps leading back to the top floor.

Coach Franklin ran both his hands over his head and let them rest behind his neck. He looked at the boys out on the ice and those on the bench, but didn't say a word. He appeared lost in thought.

"I think Coach Franklin's out to lunch," Cody muttered.

"Something's got to be done about him," Kyle added. "I'm glad Mr. Phelps had a talk with him. Maybe now he'll start thinking straight."

"Toronto!" Mitch panted, his camera tucked under his arm, "I wonder if I'll be allowed to come along to videotape the action?"

"Sure you will," Kyle said. "If we get there, that is. I don't hear Coach Franklin calling for a line change yet."

"Yeah," Cody echoed his linemate.

Ryan, who was sitting next to the boys, shook his head scornfully. "You guys can get all excited about Toronto if you want to, but that's just one tournament. I think it's more important to make sure the *whole* team enjoys the *whole* season." He pushed out his lower lip. "Personally, I like the way Coach Franklin coaches this team. He lets everybody play."

"I agree," Stu Brackett commented. "He's a fair coach."

"Fairness doesn't always win games," Kyle said. He got up and moved down the bench to the equipment bag to retape his stick, the look on his face indicating he'd had enough of the conversation. When he was out of earshot, Cody turned to Ryan.

"What's the matter with you?" he asked. It wasn't like Ryan to be so snide with his opinions.

"Nothing's the matter with me," Ryan said, "but a lot is the matter with you, ever since you and Kyle Kelley became best pals."

"What are you talking about?" Now Cody was really taken aback. This certainly was *not* the Ryan Miller he was used to, the Ryan Miller he had been friends with for years and practised hockey skills with all last year.

"I'm talking about your attitude," Ryan continued. His eyes were blazing. "Like last week — you were supposed to show up at Mitch's to watch the video of the game against the Elks. What happened?"

Cody's stomach took a sudden tumble. He'd forgotten to call Ryan to tell him he couldn't make it to Mitch's, and to ask him how he was doing after taking that shot from Kyle during practice. Obviously, Ryan was pretty upset. With Cody. And with Kyle. Cody didn't know what to say to his friend now. "I forgot," he admitted meekly.

"I'm not surprised," Ryan said. "You do have a *new* best friend now."

"That's not fair," Cody fought back.

"You're not fair," Ryan retaliated. Emotion gripped his voice. The freckles seemed to leap on his face. "You and Kyle always hog the puck, like you're the only players on this team who count."

Cody couldn't believe his ears. "That's not true!" he protested. Ryan was his friend. If it wasn't for Cody, Ryan probably wouldn't even be on the Sharks. It was Cody who had convinced him that the team was fun, that he wouldn't get hurt if he was careful. Ryan was supposed to be happy for him now that Cody had become the league's second-leading scorer. Like Mitch was. So why was Ryan being so nasty? It didn't make sense.

Cody was overcome by an urge to hurt Ryan back. He knew it wasn't the right thing to do, but Ryan had to know he couldn't walk all over him, Cody decided.

"You're just jealous because we score so many goals," Cody lashed out at his friend. He didn't feel any better for having made the comment. But the words were out now. There was nothing he could do about it.

"Sure," Ryan countered mockingly. "Whatever you say." He turned his eyes from Cody's. "But let me tell you something else — you've been a puck hog as long as I've known you."

Cody was silent. His friend's words cut through him like a knife. Anger, frustration, a sense of guilt — a whole bunch of feelings swarmed together to paralyse him.

Kyle returned and sat between Ryan and Cody. "When are we going to get back out there?" he grumbled. "I want to win this game."

Ryan turned his head away from the boys and gazed at the players on the ice. Cody looked at him, his heart beating like a jackhammer, his throat dry. He wondered what his friend was feeling right now.

Again, Kyle complained. "Is Coach Franklin going to let us back out onto the ice, or what?"

Kyle had the right attitude, Cody decided. There was a game to be played, a game to be won. Cody would prove himself out on the ice, to Ryan, to Coach Franklin, to his mom, and to everybody else.

The whistle blew. "Cody, Kyle, it's your turn," Coach Franklin called. He tapped the boys on the shoulders.

It was time to take care of business, Cody told himself.

# 6

## Hockey Heroes

As soon as he stepped onto the ice, Cody felt a jolt of electricity charge though his body. The feel of his skates against the smooth surface of the ice was like plugging him into a socket. His breathing eased, and he felt a new strength filling his bones and muscles.

The crowd was on its feet. Cody didn't know if it was his imagination or not, but he had a sense that many of the fans had their eyes on him, as if they were expecting him to make a big play, like they knew he was an important player. During his first year playing league hockey, Cody had sometimes had the feeling that the fans — and the other players — were watching him, waiting for him to make a mistake. The feeling he had now was quite different. It was as if the fans' expectations were one more thing driving him towards an inevitable result: the scoring of a goal.

The play began with the Raiders winning the face-off, and moving the puck into the Sharks' end. Ramon Rebolo made some fancy dekes and passed the Sharks' blue line uncovered. He lifted his head to look for an open player. Lone Eagle McKay was situated to his right, even closer to the net. As Stu Brackett, playing defence for the Sharks, veered towards Lone Eagle, Ramon faked a pass and bolted for the net. Ernie Gaines, playing net, turned to face Ramon, his body tensed for the shot.

Ramon lifted his stick and fired the shot. Cody watched as it blasted towards the goal. He prayed Ernie could make the save, to keep the Sharks in the game. Ernie kicked out his left leg and flopped to the ice.

Thud!

The puck thwacked against Ernie's heavy leather pads and trickled harmlessly behind the net. Stu Brackett was there to collect the loose puck and waited a moment as the Sharks readied for their offensive attack.

Cody took a deep breath. Scoring a goal was not going to be easy, he reminded himself. We'll have to work hard at it. He hustled to his spot at the left wing, waiting for the Sharks offense to take shape.

In no time, Stu shovelled a pass to Kyle, who was moving like a bullet up centre ice. Anything could happen now. Cody eyed his linemate through his plastic visor and chugged to the left, trying to stay one step ahead of the defender assigned to shadow him. But that was no easy task. The Raiders' player was taking cheap shots at Cody, slashing at his ankles and jabbing him with his elbows.

Kyle cut over the blue line, then swerved to his right. Blocked by a defender directly in front of him, he feathered a pass to Tyler on right wing.

Meanwhile, Cody decided to outsmart his defender and looped in behind the Raiders' net, skating close to the goal post, so that the defender, more interested in sticking to Cody than in looking behind him, smashed right into it and crumbled to the ice.

"I'm open!" Cody called out.

Tyler lifted his head and fed the puck quickly to Cody, who was perched safely behind the net. At the same time, Kyle charged the net. Wasting no time, Cody flew out from behind and set himself up inches away from the goalie. The goalie fell to the ground, legs opened in a wide V. Cody gripped his stick tighter as his mind raced through all the possible scenarios. He could try for a shot himself or send a pass to Kyle. He decided to go with the odds. In the next second, he flicked the puck over the goalie's pads. The puck landed smack on Kyle's stick. Kyle trapped it and sent it zooming into the wide open net.

The goal light flashed on! The Sharks had scored!

The game was tied now: RAIDERS 3, SHARKS 3.

Cody rushed to put his arms around Kyle. "Way to put it in the net, buddy!" he exclaimed.

"Way to feed it!"

As the Sharks celebrated the goal, the Raiders hung their heads. There were only twenty-three seconds left in the game, and they'd just had the victory snatched away from them.

"I knew we could do it!" Cody pronounced.

"I knew we could, too," Kyle offered. "But I'm not done yet." He flashed a wide, teasing grin. "How about you?"

Cody wasn't quite sure what his friend was getting at.

At the same time, Coach Franklin signalled from the bench for a line change. Ryan, Sean, and Noah Rivard were poised to go, their legs hanging over the boards, their sticks already sitting on the ice. Confused looks clouded their faces, as they waited for the line one players to skate to the bench.

For an instant, Cody's eyes met Ryan's, but Cody averted his glance before he could see what his friend's eyes held.

Then, following the coach's directions, Tyler skated to the bench, and Noah replaced him. But Kyle and Cody remained on the ice.

Kyle skated right in next to Cody. He lifted his visor and whispered into Cody's ear. "Just ignore the coach. Ignore everyone. Stay on the ice, and let's play this through ourselves."

"Are you sure?" Cody was nervous. It took all the courage he could muster not to look back at the Sharks' bench.

Through his helmet, though, he could hear Coach Franklin screaming for the boys to get off the ice. He didn't know what to do.

"You want to win, don't you?" Kyle coaxed him.

"Yeah," Cody answered. "But we did get the tie."

"That's not good enough. You heard what Mr. Phelps said. He wants us to win this game, so that we can play in that tournament in Toronto."

Enough thinking, Cody suddenly decided. He'd let the rush of adrenaline he felt pumping through his blood drive his actions.

"OK," he said. "Let's go for it." At the same time, out of the side of his helmet Cody could see Coach Franklin trying frantically to get the referee's attention so that he could call a time-out and straighten things out himself. But he was too late. The referee had already blown his whistle for the face-off.

There was no looking back now, Cody realized. He and Kyle were on their own. It was scary for Cody, but there was also a deliciously dangerous feeling that, for the first time in his life, he'd taken matters into his own hands. That he'd just done something that would set him apart from the pack, that would mark him as a winner, a real winner.

The Raiders' centre won the face-off. Quickly, he shot a pass through Noah's legs to Ramon, who was flying down the left wing. Ramon, in turn, zinged a pass to Lone Eagle, who crossed the blue line and headed for the net.

Obviously, the Raiders weren't satisfied with a tie, either. As he glanced up at the clock — 00:19 it read now — Cody felt a renewed respect for them.

Lone Eagle looked for someone to pass to, but Kyle had taken out the centre with a hard, open-ice bodycheck. Kyle knew that at this point in the game, the referee would only be calling the most blatant infractions.

With nobody to pass to, Lone Eagle lifted his stick for a slap shot while Ernie eased out of the net to cut down on the angle.

Behind Lone Eagle, though, Cody dove to the ice and with his stomach flat on the cold surface and his stick stretched out as far as he could possibly reach it, he somehow managed to tap the puck away from Lone Eagle.

Lone Eagle brought his stick back down to retrieve the puck, but it was too late. With his lightning speed, Kyle had moved in and stolen the puck. He was racing down the ice on a breakaway, the only thing between him and the Raiders' net were a few dozen metres of open white ice, the Raiders' goalie, and the last few seconds ticking away on the clock.

Cody propelled himself up off the ice and speeded in behind his linemate, as the rest of the players followed suit. He was gasping for breath and his muscles felt weakened, but his desire to win pushed him forward. He was heartened, too, by the knowledge that it was his playmaking that had gotten the puck to Kyle.

Meanwhile, Kyle floated on. From his vantage point, Cody couldn't help but admire him. His legs pumping, his skates slashing the ice in smooth lines, his hips swinging in a perfect rhythm, like a tiger stalking prey, Kyle looked every bit the professional hockey superstar that he would surely become.

The clock on the scoreboard read 00:11. Cody could almost feel the fans in the stands hold their breaths in anticipation of the goal. It was as if the pause button had been pressed on a VCR, and now everyone was waiting for someone to press the start button. Right now, Kyle Kelley was in control of that start button.

Kyle adjusted his shoulders and faked to the left with his head. The goalie was fooled and leaned his body to his right. In response, Kyle moved the puck to his backhand and edged even closer to the net. The goalie made a last-ditch effort to block the open end of the net, but his forward momentum had taken him too far to the right. Now, the puck zoomed over his outstretched arm. It was a picture perfect breakaway deke. Kyle's arms were on an upward swing, ready to celebrate.

What happened next was almost a blur to Cody. First, there was a loud clanging that resonated through the arena like a giant cymbal crash, as the puck, miraculously for the Raiders, hit the crossbar. The puck rebounded straight back, twirling on its side like a spinning top. The next thing Cody knew, the puck was on the blade of his stick. A mass of players, Raiders and Sharks alike, were on him by then, crushing him as if they were part of a rugby pile-up. Cody held his shoulders stiffly to fight the onslaught. He wasn't even entirely sure where the net was or where the goalie was. All he was certain of was the weight of the puck against the blade of his stick. Instinctively, he chopped at the puck. Then, straightening his back, he watched as the puck sliced through the air in slow motion and landed smack in the middle of the net.

For the second time in the last minute, the goal light behind the Raiders' net flashed on.

Elation swept over Cody like a tidal wave. He pounded his fist in the air to celebrate the goal. The fatigue of the game, the sore muscles, the emotional stress — all were suddenly lifted and he felt himself soaring across the ice in a victory lap, the cheers from the Sharks' fans in the stands washing over him.

He was a hockey hero now, and what a glorious feeling it was! He never wanted it to end.

High above him, the scoreboard was a testament to his success: RAIDERS 3, SHARKS 4.

Fans flocked from their seats to congratulate him. Players streamed off the bench to embrace him. His linemates lifted him high into the air, Kyle the first among them, holding his buddy up proudly.

"That was fantastic!" Kyle exclaimed. "Like my dad always says, 'Winners never quit.'"

"We did it! We did it!" Cody proclaimed.

Cameras flashed in their faces. Parents' hands reached out to shake theirs. Two little kids, still dressed from an earlier hockey game, approached Cody and Kyle and asked them to autograph their jerseys.

For Cody, all of this was somehow unreal, to the point where he even felt light-headed and dizzy. The warm feeling of his teammates' bodies hugging his own came as a welcome relief, a way of staying grounded amid the frenzy.

Cody looked for Ryan among the scrum of players surrounding him, congratulating him, but Ryan was nowhere to be found.

Then Mr. Phelps came waddling onto the ice in his dress shoes and suit. He beelined straight for Cody and Kyle. "Boys, boys, you did it! You certainly did it! The convenors from out east were impressed, I'll tell you that. The invitation to the Toronto tournament should be in the mail any day now. Any day now!" He patted the boys on the back and shook their hands. "Transcona is proud of you boys, that's for sure!"

At the same time, Coach Franklin made his way to the boys. "I guess we'll have to talk later on about your behaviour today, boys." Disappointment strained his voice. "What you did was not right at all."

"What's going on here?" Mr. Phelps enquired.

"It's between me and the boys, Mr. Phelps," Coach Franklin replied. Cody wasn't sure if the coach was protecting them or just saving his lecture for the privacy of the Sharks' dressing room.

Kyle spoke up then, trying to take control of the situation, Cody thought, the way he always did, especially where hockey was concerned. "Coach is all in a fuss because Cody and I stayed on for the last shift." With a straight face, Kyle looked directly into Mr. Phelps's eyes. He had guts, that was for sure, Cody thought. "But we were so caught up in the game that we didn't realize Coach had called us off the ice."

Mr. Phelps turned to Coach Franklin. "You're not going to punish these boys for winning the game, are you? That doesn't make sense."

Coach Franklin's face was serious. "I don't think we should get into this right now."

"Sure we should, Coach. This is a hockey matter, and I'm the hockey manager." Mr. Phelps's face was getting red, but Coach Franklin stood his ground.

"If you insist on an explanation, Mr. Phelps, here goes." Coach Franklin's voice was quiet but confident. "Kyle and Cody defied my instructions today and remained on the ice for the final seconds of the game, when another line was waiting their turn. The other boys, I must tell you, are very disappointed."

"But we won the game!" Cody exclaimed. A part of him was surprised that he'd just opened his mouth.

Coach Franklin shook his head, looking at Mr. Phelps. "That's not the point."

"Lighten up, Coach," Mr. Phelps gibed. "You've got some real winners here. You should be proud of them."

"I am," Coach Franklin countered. "Very proud of them. But I'm proud of the rest of the team, as well."

"Coach, the thirteen-year-old Transcona Sharks are our community club's showcase team. They're a special case. Kyle Kelley is going to make it to the NHL one day, and he might even be a superstar there. If you have to make some adjustments to your coaching policy to accommodate him, then do so. That's the way it is. That's hockey. You should know. You've been there."

"It's because I've been there that I want to take care of these boys, all of them. To make sure hockey is a *positive* experience for them."

Cody wondered just what was so bad about Coach Franklin's hockey experience.

"There's nothing more positive than winning," Mr. Phelps continued. "Call me old-fashioned, but that's the truth."

"I guess I'm not really coach of this team, then," Coach Franklin offered. His hand was nervously brushing the tip of his ear. There was something about him that reminded Cody of a gentle giant — one that had just been wounded.

"Pardon me?" Mr. Phelps asked.

Coach Franklin stirred. "Maybe I should step down from the coaching spot, is what I'm saying."

"If that's the way you feel, I'll see what I can do." Mr. Phelps didn't sound too disappointed. "I'll start looking for a new coach. Of course, it won't be easy."

"I'll stick around until the boys have a new coach," Coach Franklin replied. "Don't worry. I would never let the boys down."

"I'm glad of that," Mr. Phelps concluded. "In the meantime, count your blessings for having two players of this calibre on your squad."

Kyle couldn't repress a huge grin. Cody grinned back. As Cody saw it, Kyle had just used his clout as the superstar of the Transcona Sharks to push Coach Franklin to the sidelines. Like he'd wanted to do all along.

Suddenly, it seemed to Cody that he and Kyle had all the power in the world. That they *were* the Transcona Sharks.

# 7

# Family Matters

Arriving home after the game against the North End Raiders, Cody felt like a million bucks. He greeted Tish with a big smack on the cheeks and even called out cheerfully to his mom, "Hi, Mom, I'm home!" Things are going too well for me now, he thought, to worry about holding grudges.

"Don't tell me. You won the game, right?" Tish asked as she sat back from the kitchen table, her homework spread out neatly in front of her.

"You bet we won." Cody rummaged through the kitchen cupboards for something to eat, stopping when he discovered an opened box of granola bars. "What's more, your brother, Transcona Sharks left-winger extraordinaire, number 18, Cody Powell, scored the winning goal." He stuffed a granola bar into his mouth. "You should have heard the cheers. I was a real hockey hero tonight."

"Way to go." Tish sorted her homework into a pile and lifted it off the table. She looked at Cody, who was about to pop a second granola bar into his mouth. "Easy on the snacks, Cody," she cautioned. "Remember, you and Mom promised we'd all make dinner together tonight." She pulled a cookbook out from the shelf next to the fridge and started flipping through the pages.

"Sure, I remember. Don't you worry. After a game like tonight's I could eat a horse." Cody rubbed his belly. "I'll have plenty of room for dinner."

"Good, because as soon as Mom's finished her shower we can get started."

"As you please," Cody joked, waving his hand in a flourish like some sort of genie. "Tonight, I am at your command."

Just then, Cody's mom entered the room, looping a belt around her forest green robe. Her wet hair was combed back, away from her forehead, and her skin was pink. The soap and shampoo she'd just used filled the kitchen with fresh, clean smells.

"Good evening, Mom." Cody extended his hand. "Would you like to shake the hand of the player who scored the winning goal in tonight's game between the Transcona Sharks and the North End Raiders? A lot of other parents have already had the privilege, but I thought I'd save my warmest handshake for you."

Cody's mom took his hand and shook it. "So you're the big hero tonight, huh?" she commented. Cody wasn't sure, but he thought he sensed a trace of irony to his mom's words.

"You might say that," Cody offered, winking at Tish. He was hoping that he had misread his mom. He wanted this to be a happy occasion for the whole family.

"I heard something different about tonight's game," his mom said then. Cody knew right away that she was upset about something. "In the version I heard, you weren't so much a hero" — her eyes bore into Cody's — "as a hog."

To let her words sink in, Cody's mom matter of factly went about some kitchen business, clearing granola crumbs off the counter with her palm and replacing the box of granola bars in the cupboard.

"What are you talking about?" Cody asked, shock draining the colour from his face.

Ignoring Cody, his mom turned to Tish. "Did you decide what we're making tonight?" she asked.

"Italian-style penne with sautéed mixed vegetables," Tish replied, confused, but hoping that an argument could still somehow be avoided.

"Good, I could use some carbohydrates right about now. I've had a rough day."

Tish and Cody's mom filled the pot with water and placed it on one of the elements on the stove. She poured some olive oil in the frying pan and placed it on another element. Then she turned back to Cody, barely able to contain her scorn.

"I'll tell you what I'm talking about, Cody, and then I'll give you a chance to give me your side of the story. Because, as I see it, you have a lot of explaining to do."

Cody felt a sudden urge to cry, but he fought it back and eyed his mom crossly. Why'd she have to wreck everything that was going well for him?

"I was told that my son defied the coach's orders tonight and instead of returning to the bench after his shift, decided that he could make his own rules and stay on the ice as long as he liked." Brusquely, she handed Cody a hunk of Parmesan cheese and a grater, as if daring him to defy her now as he had Coach Franklin earlier. "And that the players whose shift it was were left stranded on the bench, unable to go out and play, like they were supposed to, like they had every right to."

"But we won!" Cody protested.

"I don't care if you won, lost, tied, or had the game postponed to the next century." She stirred the pasta in the pot with furious strokes. "At the very least, I expect my thirteen-year-old son to have the common courtesy to let his team-mates" — she raised her voice, enunciating each word long and hard — "HAVE THEIR TURNS!" She shook her head. "Didn't I teach you about taking turns somewhere way back about the same time we had a lesson in sharing? I think you were four years old at the time."

"Mom!"

"Is it the truth, or isn't it?"

"Who told you this?" Cody fought back. He knew very well who was behind all this, and he wasn't too happy about it. He'd told his mom that dating Coach Franklin would cause problems. Now it was his turn to lash out.

"That's not important," Cody's mom replied. "What's important is your behaviour."

Cody felt backed into a corner. Everything had come crashing in on him, and he wasn't going to take it. He'd walked into this house a few minutes ago feeling on top of the world. Now, anger boiled up inside him like a seething volcano about to blow.

"It was Coach Franklin, wasn't it?" As much as he'd tried to keep them back, Cody now felt tears burning his eyes. "I told you dating him would ruin things for me on the Sharks. Why couldn't you just have stayed out of my business?"

Cody's mom pulled her robe tighter around her body. "It wasn't Joe Franklin, Cody."

"I don't believe you!" Cody was crying openly now. His voice tore through the kitchen like a cat's nighttime wailing.

"It wasn't Joe Franklin," Cody's mom repeated. "Believe it or not, Cody, I have respected and will continue to respect your wish that my dating Joe Franklin doesn't get in the way of your hockey. For your information, we never discuss your hockey games."

"You're lying, Mom!" Cody roared. "I know you're lying!" He stormed to the back door and sat at the steps leading to the basement, pulling on his boots.

"Cody, where are you going?" Tish called out. She was crying, and her face was twisted with fear. "You guys promised we'd cook dinner together tonight." She wiped at her eyes. "You promised."

Cody kept his head down. "I'm sorry, Tish, but I can't stay," he snapped. "I'm sorry."

Cody's mom moved to the back door, one arm wrapped protectively around Tish. "Cody, please don't leave now." Her voice cracked. "It's cold outside. You'll freeze."

"You lied, Mom," Cody answered back. He threw on his winter coat.

"No, Cody, I didn't lie." Cody's mom reached her hand out to touch her son's shoulders, but he turned away to avoid her. "It wasn't Joe Franklin who told me what you did at tonight's game. It was Francine Miller, Ryan's mother. She called me as soon as Ryan got home after the game. He was crying, saying you and Kyle had ruined the game for him, that you'd taken away his chance to play his shift. He says he's thinking of quitting the team now, because of you and Kyle."

Now, Cody wished he hadn't pressed his mom to tell him who had called her about tonight's game. When he thought it was Coach Franklin, he had been angry, but he had felt justified in his anger. This feeling now was worse, much worse.

Cody looked back at his mom for a second. Her face was anguished, but it also held the promise of comfort. Part of him wished he could run back to her and bury himself deep in her arms. The other part wanted to get as far away as possible from this place.

He stepped outside into the cold air and slammed the door hard behind him.

He wasn't sure, though, whether he had just slammed the door in anger at his mom, or in disgust at himself.

# 8

# Wilted in Winnipeg

Snow pelted from the sky in tiny flakes that prickled Cody's face. He pulled his collar higher over his neck and continued walking, his boots tattooing a careless pattern on the sidewalk.

Cody had no idea where he was going. Normally, after an argument with his mom, or when he needed to get out of the house for whatever reason, he would head straight for the snow fort he, Mitch, Ryan, and Ernie had built in the empty field behind Ernie's house. They called it "The Igloo" because they had used blocks of hard-packed snow to build the walls. He knew he wasn't welcome there now, though. Not if Ryan had succeeded in convincing the others that Cody was a jerk.

Suddenly, the thought occurred to Cody that what he had just done, the way he had left home — slamming the door on his mom — was a lot like the way his dad used to leave the house after an argument with his mom. He'd always hated that about his dad, the way he used to just leave like that — one day, finally, for good. And now he'd gone and done very much the same thing. A cold chill ran down his spine.

Ahead of him, Cody saw rows of clapboard houses decorated with strings of coloured Christmas lights. Some houses featured lights that were strung to form a huge star or candy cane, and a few houses even had Santa Clauses riding in miniature sleighs on their snow-covered front lawns.

What if all of this, Cody wondered, this whole neighbour-hood of mine, all dressed up now for the Christmas season, was just some ornament, the kind you bought in a gift shop and shook real hard to make the tiny flakes inside look like snow? He felt like that. Like some insignificant character in someone else's grand scheme. Like whenever he thought he could make something happen right in his life, someone or something would come along to shake things up, teasing him for even thinking he had a chance to make some sort of difference.

In the distance a train screeched to a stop, the brakes hissing loudly. The smell of a wood fire burning in someone's fireplace filled the air with a sweet tang. Smoke from chimneys spiralled into the sky, formulating an indecipherable secret language.

Life was strange, Cody decided, painfully strange. Right now he was feeling low, lower than he had felt in a long, long time, and he was mixed up about what was right and what was wrong. Meanwhile, his dad, his very own dad, right this very instant, was thousands of kilometres away, in some other province, in some other city, in some other house — in some other world, really — laughing, for all Cody knew, at a joke on TV, or getting ready for bed, or even talking to one of Della's kids about one of *their* problems.

That's what is most strange, Cody thought: my dad's in one place, and I'm here in another. Cody didn't so much resent his dad's absence as realize suddenly how little sense it made, at least for him, and for Tish. There were so many little, everyday things in their lives, not to mention big things, that their dad missed out on, not because he didn't care about Cody and Tish, but simply because he wasn't *there* with them. Part of being a family was in *being*, as in *being around, being there*. You just couldn't *be* that way when you were halfway across the country.

It would be good to have his dad around right now, Cody couldn't help thinking as he wiped the wet snow from his face. Maybe things would be different then. Somehow, they would just have to be different.

\*\*\*

Cody decided to go call on Kyle. Without realizing it, he'd already walked more than half of the way there, crossing the tracks into the neighbourhood of larger, newer houses where Ryan and Kyle both lived. Cody had never been to Kyle's place before, but he knew where it was, and he felt like the two of them were now good enough friends that he could show up and ask to hang out for awhile.

Part of him hoped that seeing Kyle would make him feel good again about his accomplishments at the hockey game earlier that day.

When he reached the crescent where Kyle lived, he saw his friend's house immediately. It stood at the rear of the bend, brick-fronted with a swirling roof that made the house look something like a castle.

At the front steps, Cody was kind of nervous. He wondered how Kyle would react to his visit and if he would have time to spend with him. Finally, Cody rang the doorbell. It chimed, like the bells of a clock tower.

To his relief, Kyle answered the door. He was wearing his coat and boots and looked like he was just heading out the door himself.

"Cody!" Kyle exclaimed. "Where have you been? I've been calling your place for over an hour. Lanya and Kirsten are waiting for us at the store."

"What?"

"The girls called me up tonight and said they were free. I told them we'd meet at 7 Eleven. I didn't know it would take so long to track you down. I'd just given up." He zipped his coat. "But you're here now, so let's get going." Kyle put his arm around Cody's shoulder to lead him out the door.

But right before they stepped outside, a woman's voice came trailing after them. "Kyle, where do you think you're going at this hour?" Soon Cody heard footsteps approaching. Kyle stopped in his tracks.

Kyle's mom appeared at the door. She looked at Cody, smiled pleasantly, then turned to her son. In her hand she was holding a cordless phone that she had just switched off.

"I'm going to the store for a while, just to hang out," Kyle answered.

Kyle's mom glanced at her watch. Cody noticed that it was thick and shiny, with a gold and silver wristband. "But you haven't spent any time studying yet. You have a math test this week, don't forget."

Kyle's dad joined his wife at the front door, holding a rumpled newspaper and wearing leather slippers. He was tall and handsome, with wavy salt-and-pepper hair.

"Let the boy celebrate his comeback victory, Tanis," he stated.

"Glen, Kyle needs to study for that test. Mathematics is his weakest subject." She turned to Kyle. "Frankly, honey, all your school marks are suffering this year. "

"Mom!" Kyle protested.

"Well, it's the truth," Kyle's mom said.

Cody had never stopped to think about what kind of student Kyle might be. As far as he was concerned, Kyle was just a hockey superstar, period. Now he realized Kyle had his weaknesses, just like anybody else.

"Tanis, ease up on the boy," Kyle's dad stated, draping his arm over Kyle's shoulders. "He's caught up in his hockey right now."

Kyle's mom shook her head. "Hockey's all you two seem to be talking about this year. Hockey's important, granted, and Kyle has a special talent, but there are other things in life. Like school."

"Kyle has the smarts, he just hasn't taken to books. Just like his dad." Kyle's dad motioned with his hand to the beautiful cathedral-ceilinged home behind them. "And I haven't done too poorly for myself."

"Glen!"

"I know, I know, Tanis. I should be encouraging Kyle to do well in school. You're right. I just think he'll get around to it, in his own time."

"I will, Mom," Kyle broke in. He seemed embarrassed to be talked about like this in front of Cody. "In fact, I promise I'll study as soon as I get back tonight." He flashed a warm smile at his mom. "Can I go now?"

"OK," Kyle's mom replied. She wagged her head. "But be back by ten. I mean it."

"Don't worry," Kyle answered. Then, quickly, he leapt down the stairs. "Let's get going," he called to Cody. "Parents can be a real drag."

***

At the 7 Eleven, Kyle and Cody met Lanya and Kirsten. The four of them had a Slurpee each and took turns playing the video games at the back of the store. It was just the kind of mindless activity that Cody needed right now.

The cashiers behind the counter were listening to the radio. Cody had to snicker — they were listening to the *Dr. Muldoon Show*. He wondered if Tish was listening to the program, too, or maybe she was already in bed.

Suddenly, one of the cashiers started shouting, "The announcer just said the next call's from Winnipeg! Can you believe it? From Winnipeg!" She turned the radio louder, filling the store with the soothing voice of Dr. Muldoon. The other cashiers gathered around the speaker to listen closely. So did Cody, Kyle, Lanya, and Kirsten. It wasn't often that Dr. Muldoon took a caller from Winnipeg.

"We have a caller now from Winnipeg, Canada," Dr. Muldoon said. "She doesn't want her real name used on the air, so she's asked to be called Wilted in Winnipeg."

"Wilted in Winnipeg!" Lanya repeated. "I love it!"

The radio program continued. "Well, Wilted in Winnipeg, what's troubling you? Or should I say, what's wilting you?"

"It's my family," the caller explained. "We're just not getting along. I'm worried that something terrible is going to happen. Again."

The voice was young, and Cody knew it sounded familiar, very familiar.

"How old are you, dear?" Dr. Muldoon asked tenderly. "You sound very young."

"I'm eight years old," the caller replied. Now Cody was sure he knew whose voice it was. His heart almost stopped in his chest.

"What are you worried is going to happen?"

"Well, when I was still six years old my mom and dad were divorced." Tish's voice cracked. The cashiers nodded their heads at one another in sympathy. "That wasn't very good, but I think my brother and I have finally learned to live with it. Last Christmas we visited my dad. He lives in British Columbia with a new family."

"That must have been tough," Dr. Muldoon prompted Tish.

"It was," Tish said. "I just wanted my mom and dad to stay together, and now I have to learn to live with them being apart. It doesn't make it easy for us to be a family."

"Has something happened recently to make things worse?"

"Yes," Tish answered. "My mom's started dating. It's nothing serious, I don't think, but she's gone out a few times with this man, and I'm worried that if she really likes him she might not want to get back together with my father again."

Dr. Muldoon cut in. "That probably wouldn't happen anyhow, dear. As unfortunate as it is, your parents must have gotten divorced for a reason."

"I know," Tish continued, "my mom keeps telling me that, and so does my brother."

"How is your brother with all this?"

"He's been OK, especially with me, but today he got into a fight with my mom, and he left the house" — Tish sniffled, holding back a cry — "the same way my dad used to leave the house after he fought with my mom."

Cody dropped his head to his chest and rubbed his temples. He should never have left the way he did tonight. He hated himself for what he had done.

Tish went on. "What I'm really afraid of is that we'll stop being a family. That's all I want, for us to be a family. Mom and Dad promised us that we could still be a family when they got divorced, but it's not turning out that way."

There was a click over the airwaves, and the phone line went dead.

"Are you still there, caller? Are you on the line?"

There was no answer.

Dr. Muldoon took a deep breath, on the air. "That call speaks for itself," she said. "I can't add a word. I just hope that somehow things turn out right for that girl." The program switched to a loud commercial.

Cody felt like he'd just woken from a bad dream. He lifted his head. "I'm sorry," he said to his friends. "It's really late. I've got to get home."

"Are you all right?" Lanya asked.

But Cody was already outside the store. He stepped into the cold, the wet snow spitting on him from the sky. He was crying freely now, streams of tears that the cold north wind froze in jagged lines on his face.

Some hockey hero I am, he thought.

# 9

## A Pre-Game Meeting

For the big game the following week against the St. Vital Marauders, Cody arrived at Lord Strathcona Arena an hour early because Mr. Phelps and Coach Franklin had called a special team meeting. Of course, by now everybody on the Transcona Sharks knew that tonight they could end up with a new coach for the rest of the season. Cody wasn't sure what he wanted. He was beginning to understand that the other players on the team deserved equal time on the ice, even if they didn't score as many goals as Kyle and Cody's line, but he still wasn't overly fond of Coach Franklin. A team needs a coach who is tough and smart, and who can control the players. And who isn't going out with my mom, Cody thought.

The arena was empty and quiet. His duffel bag weighing down his shoulders, Cody walked up to the display case at the front of the arena. Before games he often liked to admire the trophies, banners, and framed photographs inside. He gazed now at last year's photo of the twelve-year-olds' team. He was there, standing on the far left in the second row, wearing for the most part the oversized hockey equipment he'd borrowed from Ryan. He remembered how nervous he had been at his first practice, how lost he had felt in his first game. He'd come a long way since then, that was for sure. He was a better player — smarter, tougher, faster. He wondered, though, if he was a better person.

For one thing, he was beginning to see that he'd ignored his long-time friendship with Ryan just to win favour with Kyle. For another, listening to Tish's call to the *Dr. Muldoon Show*, Cody had realized that he should never forget that he wasn't the only one in his family going through difficult times.

When he descended to the dressing room, Cody found several of his teammates sitting at the benches, split into their usual groups. Nobody was saying much, as if they were saving the talking for the meeting. Cody crossed to his locker and laid down his duffel bag. He looked around for Kyle, but didn't see him. At the far end of the room, though, he saw Ryan sitting with Ernie and Stu Brackett. They were talking among themselves, but Cody noticed their eyes discreetly glance his way a few times.

He wondered what they were saying about him. He hoped there was some way for him to earn their trust again.

Soon the entire team showed up, even Kyle, who took a seat next to Cody. After that, Coach Franklin came in, with Mr. Phelps following him. All the boys in the room stopped what they were doing and looked at the two men, searching for clues as to what the final decision about the coaching situation would be. But both men wore stony expressions.

"Boys, I called you to this meeting today because this team, although it hasn't lost a single game this season, is suffering," Coach Franklin began. He gripped a stick horizontally in his hands, so tensely it looked as if he might snap it into two pieces at any second. "As you all know, during our last game, there was an incident in which two of our players showed very poor sportsmanship at the expense of others on the team." Cody dropped his eyes, not wanting to know who was staring at him now, with contempt. "We have to find a way to make sure something like that doesn't happen again."

Mr. Phelps gave Coach Franklin a rebuking glance. "You youngsters must understand that you are fortunate enough this year to be a part of a very special team." He held up some newspaper clippings featuring the Transcona Sharks. "This is more than just a winning team. This is a team that can compete with the best teams your age in Canada. If we do things right, we can really make it big." He broke into a huge grin. "I've already received an invitation for us to play in an interprovincial tournament in Toronto in March. And, just a few moments ago, I was informed that at tonight's game one of the fans sitting in the stands with your parents and grandparents and brothers and sisters will be a scout with the Calgary Flames."

Across the bench, eyes opened wide and jaws dropped. The team let out a collective "Wow!" Kyle turned to Cody and high-fived him. The idea of a scout watching tonight's game dazzled Cody. Imagine a scout liking the way I play enough to recommend me to an NHL team! he thought. Wouldn't that be something!

Coach Franklin cleared his throat loudly to regain the boys' attention. "As exciting as that news may be, we still have to face the fact that this team is being pulled in two different directions, and many of you are not happy. We're not going to make it to the end of the season, let alone to some tournament in Toronto, if we continue like this. Something must be done to keep this team together." He turned to Mr. Phelps. "Mr. Phelps has suggested that perhaps that 'something' should be my stepping down as coach."

"But ..." Stu Brackett blurted.

"This isn't something I necessarily want to do," Coach Franklin cut in, "but if I see that it's best for this team, then I won't hesitate a minute."

"Who would be our coach?" Kyle asked.

"Mr. Phelps has made some enquiries with some of the parents, asking if they'd like to coach this team," Coach Franklin said. "Of course, if that doesn't work out, he has indicated that he could coach the team himself."

"All right!" Kyle exclaimed.

"No way!" Stu protested.

"Boys, boys," Coach Franklin continued. "We haven't made any decisions yet. That's why we called today's meeting. To see how you all feel about this team and what needs to be done to keep it together."

"We need Mr. Phelps to coach us," Kyle called out. "He knows what it takes to win."

"We need to discipline players who don't follow the rules," Ryan retorted. He eyeballed Kyle and Cody.

Coach Franklin put his hand out to ask for silence. "I've been coaching this team with my main goal being to let all of you play as much as possible. Maybe that's not what all of you want."

Kyle put his hand up, and Coach Franklin nodded for him to speak. "I don't think there's anything wrong with letting the best players have the most ice time. It's done all the time in the NHL. When the Rangers are down, they put Gretzky on the ice. When the Avalanche need a goal, they double-shift Joe Sakic. That's just the way it is."

"Maybe that's the way it is in the NHL," Ryan pointed out, "where the players get paid to play, but in this league it's us kids — well, our parents — who pay so that we can play, and I say that if we're paying we shouldn't have to spend our time on the bench. That's what my mother says."

"I don't care if I have to sit on the bench," Noah put in. "If it means this team gets a free trip to Toronto, then I'm all for it." He grinned. "The CN Tower, Wonderland — Toronto's the coolest!"

"I'd rather see everyone on the team get equal time on the ice," Ernie countered, adjusting his goalie pads. "That's why we're here. To play hockey."

Suddenly, Cody couldn't help wondering whether tonight's meeting would solve anything. The team seemed evenly split over the issue. In any case, he didn't dare say a word. He didn't want to be accused of being a hog again, especially not by Ryan.

"I like Coach Franklin," Ryan continued. "He's a fair coach who cares about his players more than he cares about winning. This is my first year playing league hockey, and I'm really enjoying it because of Coach Franklin."

"Ditto," Ernie added.

"If this team doesn't want to compete with the best in the league, then I don't want to be a part of it," Kyle said. As if to emphasize his point, he began unlacing his skates. "I know that there are other teams I can sign up with that would be happy to have me."

"Go ahead!" Ryan dared him.

Mr. Phelps stepped forward then. "Hold on, boys, hold on! This is the kind of talk we don't need tonight or any other night. Please, let's not make this personal."

"It *is* personal," Ryan continued. "And I'll tell you what. If Coach Franklin's not the coach of this team, I quit."

"Same here!" Ernie shouted.

"Me, too!" Stu added.

"Boys! Boys! Boys!" Coach Franklin interrupted.

"We have to pull together," Mr. Phelps persisted. "This is a big night. The Marauders are a good team. If we can beat them, we know we're probably the best in the city." He pulled on his chin. "I have a suggestion."

"What is it?" Coach Franklin asked. Lines of worry had ringed the bottom of his eyes.

"What if we coach the team together, at least for tonight's game?"

"I'm not sure that would be a wise decision," Coach Franklin admitted.

"Do you have anything better to suggest?"

Coach Franklin turned to the players. "Boys, does anyone have a problem with Mr. Phelps's idea?"

None of the boys nodded or shook his head. The room was gripped in silence.

Coach Franklin faced Mr. Phelps. "Well, then, it looks like you'll have two coaches for tonight's game," he concluded. "This should be an interesting experiment. Let's hope for the best."

"Come on, boys, put your right hands out and let's send up three cheers for the Transcona Sharks," Mr. Phelps commanded. "Show some team spirit!"

Lamely, the players on the team put their hands together and chanted "Sharks! Sharks! Sharks!" Their voices were so weak, nobody outside the dressing room could have heard them.

We can hope for the best, Cody thought, but two coaches for the Transcona Sharks might just be a recipe for disaster.

# 10

# Hockey Night in Transcona

The tension was so thick on the Sharks' bench, you could slice it with a hockey stick. Fans were piling into the arena by the dozens. Cody noticed Kyle sneak a peak at the stands every so often, trying to figure out which of the fans was the Calgary Flames' hockey scout. Meanwhile, the St. Vital Marauders took the ice for their pre-game skate and looked strong and determined. They had their sharpshooters back from last season, Ed Danko and Miles Pilski, and a bunch of new players that rounded off the roster with a good mix of talent.

Mr. Phelps and Coach Franklin were exchanging hushed words, the expressions on their faces less than friendly. Every so often, Coach Franklin scribbled a few hurried notes on his clipboard. Obviously, the two men were trying to figure out a game plan that would work for the Transcona Sharks.

In a few moments, Coach Franklin clapped his hands to get the team's attention. "Boys, we're going to do something a little bit different tonight," he announced. "It's something Mr. Phelps and I hope will help pull this team back together."

The boys on the bench turned their heads, their eyes riveted on Coach Franklin.

"We're going to mix up some of the lines, put a few of you out there with new players at your side, just to see how things turn out." Coach Franklin read from his rough notes. "To begin with, line one will consist of Cody, Kyle, and Ryan, and line two will have Sean, Tyler, and Noah."

Cody couldn't believe his ears! Ryan and Kyle were first-class enemies, and he and Ryan weren't getting along so well either, right now. How would a line with the three of them work out?

Tonight's game kept shaping up into a disaster just waiting to happen.

The buzzer to start the game was a wake-up call to the Transcona Sharks. It was now or never for them — either they pulled together or the team would end up smashed into fragments.

Cody's line was the first to take the ice. As they prepared for the opening face-off, Kyle skated in behind Cody. "Do your best to keep the puck away from Ryan," he whispered into Cody's ear. "He could make us look bad."

Cody nodded, but inside he wondered if that was such a good idea. Excluding Ryan from the action would pull the team further apart. Then again, if the Sharks wanted to win this game, it was probably the one-two combination of Kyle and Cody who could do it.

The Marauders won the face-off and began their offensive. They were a well-organized, obviously well-coached squad. Miles controlled the puck while Ed darted towards the net. Sensing something was about to happen, Cody back-pedalled to help stop the rush.

Out of nowhere, a bulky Marauders' forward came flying towards Cody, looking for a pass from Miles. Cody stood his ground. If the Marauders' player wanted to reach the puck, he'd have to go through Cody to do it.

That prospect, however, didn't seem to bother the Marauders' forward. As the puck slid across the ice, he lunged forward, intent on steamrolling through Cody. Cody readied himself for the blow. But it never came. Kyle had arrived on the scene, using his shoulders to deliver a textbook check on the Marauders' forward, who fell, scrambling, to the ice. Cody picked up the loose puck and cleared it, sending it over the boards and into the stands.

"Thanks," Cody said to Kyle as soon as the referee had blown his whistle. Again, Kyle had come through for him.

"Don't mention it," Kyle replied. He looked up at the stands. "Do you think the scout caught that one? I want him to know I can play tough."

"He's probably on the phone right now to Calgary, making arrangements to sign you up on the Flames," Cody joked.

"My dad would sure be proud of me then, " Kyle said. His eyes, Cody noticed, were sharp and intense. Hockey means a lot to him, Cody thought, more than it means to most of the other players on the Transcona Sharks. For Kyle, it means proving to his father that he's a winner.

After the face-off, Lyall Noyes, on the Sharks' defence, took control of the puck and sped it towards the Marauders' end of the ice. Lyall searched for an open forward. At the same time, Ryan hollered from the right wing. His defender was allowing him a lot of space, as if he were more interested in keeping his eyes on Kyle than covering Ryan. In the next moment, Lyall flicked a pass to Ryan. Ryan collected the puck onto his blade and skated forward. He lifted his head high, looking to make a play. Cody called for the pass. Ryan leaned down to make it. But from behind Ryan, a Marauders' defender appeared. Poking his stick forward, the defender robbed Ryan of the puck.

In a matter of seconds, the Marauders were on a three-on-two attack. Fortunately for the Sharks, Ernie made a diving save to keep the game scoreless.

Coach Franklin called for a line change. At the bench, Kyle started hollering at Lyall. "Are you crazy? I was wide open! What'd you go and pass to Ryan for?"

"He was more open than you were," Lyall answered back.

"Well, a lot of good passing to him did. We almost got scored on."

"Boys! Boys! Please settle down," Coach Franklin called out. "The game has just started. Try to hold back on the bickering."

"I could've made a great play out there. Just tell these guys to pass to me," Kyle grumbled. Again he gazed up at the stands, as if wondering what kind of evaluation the Calgary Flames' scout was giving him.

Meanwhile, Cody looked along the bench at Ryan, who was sitting with his head flopped down over his chest. Cody could tell that Ryan felt bad about flubbing that last play, and probably even worse for being ridiculed about it by Kyle.

The game continued, with neither team scoring. Ernie was hot in net, keeping the Marauders from earning a goal. Meanwhile, the Sharks were playing shoddy hockey. Kyle, Cody noticed, wasn't quite himself. Usually, he was cool as a cucumber out on the ice, but tonight there was a nervousness to his movements. He tried to force a few plays, and he took two stupid penalties. At one point, Mr. Phelps had to tell him to calm down and not think about the scout out in the stands. "We can't have our star player spending half the game in the penalty box," he warned.

\*\*\*

With the first period winding down, Kyle, Cody, and Ryan took the ice for one more attempt to score a goal. Kyle appeared determined to pick up the pace of the game. As he hunkered down for the face-off, shoulders forward, stick at the ready, he looked to Cody a lot like the shark on his team jersey.

Sure enough, Kyle won the face-off, his brute strength overpowering the Marauders' centre. His skates shooting ice shavings behind him, he rocketed forward, electrifying the entire arena. If the scout is watching now, Cody thought, he's taking notes like crazy.

Coming to a stop just inside the blue line, Kyle waited for Cody to position himself near the Marauders' crease. Then he fired a pass across the ice. The puck slipped past two defenders, and was headed straight for Cody's stick. But Ryan, who had also moved in on the offensive, found the puck on his stick first. Quickly, he one-timed the puck at the goalie. But the goalie's glove hand darted out like a serpent's tongue and made the save.

Kyle stormed at Ryan in a rage. "Why'd you get in the way of that pass? It was meant for Cody!"

"Sorry," Ryan replied, keeping his head down. Cody could tell his friend felt awful. "The puck landed on my stick so I took a shot, that's all."

Kyle shook his head. "Well, stay out of the play next time. How about that?"

Cody edged closer to Ryan. "The goalie made a good save. It wasn't your fault." But Ryan didn't seem ready to listen to Cody. He skated away to his position, waiting for the face-off.

Cody turned to Kyle. "He had a good shot on net," he said.

"And he ruined it," Kyle said shortly. He looked up at the clock: 1:23 remained in the first period. "We still have time to jump ahead. Just keep the puck away from Ryan."

After the face-off, the play moved into the Sharks' zone. Danko shot from inside the blue line, but Ernie made the save. Lyall picked up the rebound for the Sharks and looked for an open forward. He found Ryan and slid the puck his way. Ryan took the puck in and made his move. Cody could tell he was nervous, though, and self-conscious. In the next moment, as the Marauders pulled back to set up on defence, Kyle skated right up to Ryan and simply stripped him of the puck, leaving Ryan with a bewildered expression on his face. His own teammate had just stolen the puck from him! Meanwhile, Kyle rushed forward.

Cody knew what Kyle had just done wasn't fair, but there was nothing he could do about it right now. Kyle was bringing the puck into the Marauders' end and he needed backup. Sure enough, Kyle wheeled towards the net and then, when he found the Marauders building a seamless wall in front of him, dropped a pretty pass back to Cody. Cody leaned down hard into the puck and sent it flying over the pile of Marauders' defenders and into the net.

A goal!

The arena went wild, like a pinball machine lighting up after a big score. Kyle skated over to congratulate Cody. "See, I told you we could do it," he said. "I'm feeling hot now."

Cody smiled. "Great pass!" he enthused. He looked over at Ryan, who was skating off the ice with sagging shoulders. Cody was thrilled about the goal he'd just scored, but at the same time he felt bad that Ryan had been pushed aside in order to make the play.

There must be a better way for this team to work together, he thought.

At the Sharks' bench, Cody accepted more congratulations from the rest of the players, Coach Franklin and Mr. Phelps. He sat down and looked up at the scoreboard. SHARKS 1, MARAUDERS 0, it read. He took off his helmet and poured water over his face, then closed his eyes and sat back to drink in the moment, to sort through his thoughts.

After a minute or so of relaxing in a dream-like state, Cody felt a tap on his shoulder. It was Coach Franklin. For a change, there was a bit of a smile pasted on his face.

"There's someone here who wants to see you," he said.

"What?" Cody was confused.

Coach Franklin wagged his index finger for Cody to follow him. Cody rose from his seat and walked across the length of the bench, his legs knocking into his teammates' knees.

"Who wants to see me?" he asked the coach.

"It's a surprise," Coach Franklin replied.

A surprise? Cody thought. Suddenly, he had an idea of who it was. The scout! Cody's heart raced with anticipation. The scout had seen Cody's goal and was coming down to tell him he was going to mention Cody to the coaching staff of the Calgary Flames. He'd probably tell Cody about how much of a sacrifice hockey could be, but that he thought Cody had the raw talent to make it in the NHL. Cody couldn't believe his luck!

He reached the end of the bench and turned around as Coach Franklin returned to his spot at the corner of the bench. Cody couldn't see anyone. What's going on? he thought. Is this a joke or something?

Suddenly, a face popped up from behind one of the seats in the row just behind the Sharks' bench.

"Surprise!" came the familiar voice.

It was Cody's father.

# 11

# A Face-Off Between Friends

"Dad!"

"Cody, how are you?" His dad rushed to wrap his strong arms around Cody. Cody had spoken to his father at least once a week since he moved to Kamloops, but it had been almost a year since he had actually been with him, near him. He snuggled in closer now so that all his senses could appreciate the novelty of his father's presence.

"How long have you been here?"

"Just in time to catch your goal!" Cody's dad beamed. He kept his arms on Cody's shoulders, looking him fully in the face. "That was fantastic. I was really proud."

"How'd you get here? Are you going to stay long?"

Cody's dad winced. "I'm afraid I'm only going to be in town long enough to watch this game. Then I have to head back to the airport. Your mom said she would drive you and Tish there to see me off."

"You mean tonight?"

Cody's dad glanced at his watch. "At 9:45 p.m., to be precise." His dad took a deep swallow. "I'm on my way to Toronto for a union convention, but I made arrangements to have a few hours layover time here in Winnipeg, so that I can see you and Tish and personally deliver your Christmas gifts."

"Thanks, Dad." Cody stepped back to gaze at his dad. He looked cool in a plaid shirt and tight blue jeans, younger, Cody thought, than most of his friends' dads. For some crazy reason, suddenly Cody felt like calling out to his teammates, "Hey, it's my dad!" and showing him off to everybody.

"Your mom told me you were playing here tonight," Cody's dad went on, "so I rushed right over. Tish is at karate class."

"We're winning!" Cody exclaimed, glancing at the scoreboard. The last few seconds of the opening period were winding down. "I guess you know that."

"I sure do." Cody's dad took a sweeping look around Lord Strathcona Arena. "The old place hasn't changed too much from when I used to play here. Of course, I was never as much of a goal scorer as you are. I was always one of the tough guys on the team." He nodded then towards Coach Franklin. "Nowhere near as tough as Joe Franklin, though. We used to call him 'the Bruiser.'"

The buzzer sounded ending the period. The players on both teams skated to their benches to take a break from the action. Cody took the opportunity to remain a few more minutes with his dad.

"You know Coach Franklin?" Cody gasped.

"Doesn't everybody in Transcona?" Cody's dad chuckled to himself. "I guess a lot of time has passed since those days. Anyhow, Joe Franklin was one of the toughest, meanest guys on the ice. That's how he got his contract with Fort Wayne in the International League."

"Well, he's totally against violence now. He takes a fit if any of us guys gets a little too rough."

"I can understand that," Cody's dad said, nodding his head slowly. "After the accident and all."

"What accident?" Cody asked. "Was he hurt real bad by somebody?" Cody and Kyle had suspected as much all along.

Cody's dad shook his head. "No, it was the other way around. I remember reading about it in the local paper. Everybody was talking about it. Joe hammered some guy into the boards. The guy lost consciousness and had to be driven by an ambulance to the hospital. He almost died. Joe quit the team the very same day. Spent most of his time visiting the guy in the hospital until the guy got better. And he never played organized hockey after that, at least not that I can remember."

Cody remained silent. There was nothing to say. He finally understood why Coach Franklin was so adamant about the boys playing clean, safe hockey. Maybe, Cody thought, he and Kyle had misjudged Coach Franklin.

Cody's dad patted Cody on the shoulder. "Listen, you'd better get back to your team, now. Don't worry about me. I'll watch the rest of the game and then take a cab to the airport. Your mom said she'd bring you and Tish by 8:30."

"OK, Dad," Cody said. He couldn't wait to see his dad after the game. Meanwhile, for the first time in his life, he would have his dad around to watch him play league hockey. It was a dream come true. "See you later."

*** 

The second period was more of the same as the first. Both teams played hard, but the Sharks seemed stiff and confused. The new lines they were trying out were taking some adjusting to, and nobody was able to click for another goal. Kyle was getting more and more frustrated with Ryan, blaming him every time the boys had a shift and the puck failed to land in the net.

The Marauders, however, did manage to score once, on a breakaway slapshot from Miles. As the buzzer blasted to signal the end of the second period, the score was tied: SHARKS 1, MARAUDERS 1.

If Kyle seemed hopelessly frustrated by the game, Mr. Phelps was worse. He was pacing along the bench, hands in his pants' pockets, his neck twitching madly. Every time the Sharks missed a scoring opportunity, he'd kick at the wooden boards in front of the bench.

"I don't know what's wrong with me tonight," Kyle complained to Cody as the two boys waited out another shift. "The puck's just not going into the net for me."

"We're all having a tough game," Cody answered.

"At least you got a goal," Kyle mentioned. His eyes drifted upwards to the stands. "The scout saw you score, but he still hasn't seen me get a goal."

"But you made a great pass. That's why I scored."

"I want the scout to know that I've got good hands, that I can put the puck into the net."

"You'll do it," Cody offered. "There's still a full period left. In that time you could get six goals."

"Not tonight," Kyle shook his head. He looked along the bench. "I think the line changes are to blame. I don't like playing on the same line as Ryan. I'd rather have Tyler on right wing."

"Come on, Ryan's played all right tonight," Cody said. "It's not his fault we're not scoring."

"He stinks," Kyle spat out. "I don't want him playing on our line, and I'm going to do something about it."

"What are you talking about?"

"I'm asking for another right-winger on our line," Kyle explained. "Tyler would be great. Or Sean. Even Noah would be better than Ryan. I know Mr. Phelps will back us on this. Especially if we both ask."

"But what about Ryan?" Cody asked.

"What about him?"

"He'll feel terrible if we ask to have him taken off our line."

"You're not going soft on me now, Cody, are you?" There was fire in Kyle's eyes. "I mean, we have to win this game. You're either with the winners or with the losers, and Ryan's a loser."

Kyle rose from the bench and walked towards Mr. Phelps. Cody hesitated, his heart beating out of control.

"Are you coming or not?" Kyle pressed, looking back at Cody, who was frozen in his seat.

# 12

# A Tough Decision

Cody didn't know what to do. Ryan deserved another chance. He hadn't played poorly, and even if he had, it was cruel to shove him aside now. You didn't do that to a teammate, or to a friend. On the other hand, Cody knew that if he stuck with Kyle, they could probably recapture their goal-scoring magic and win this game. They would be hockey heroes once again.

"Don't you want to win this game?" Kyle demanded.

"Of course I do." Cody responded.

"Then?"

"I don't know."

Still, Cody was unable to move from his seat.

"I guess I'll have to do this alone, then," Kyle stated. "Thanks a lot."

Part of Cody wanted to shoot up and follow Kyle, to show him that he did support him, that he would be there for him. But he couldn't do that to Ryan, couldn't betray him like that. And besides, Cody decided, what Kyle was asking wasn't right. Not at all.

In a moment, the buzzer sounded to start the third period. Cody could see Mr. Phelps and Coach Franklin talking animatedly with Kyle. Then they moved along the bench to where Cody was sitting.

"We're putting Kyle and you on a line with Tyler," Mr. Phelps announced. "Ryan can play with Sean and Noah." He put his arm on Kyle's shoulders. "You guys are out there first, so get going."

Cody looked at Mr. Phelps and then to Coach Franklin, who didn't look too happy with this decision.

"I don't know what we're going to tell Ryan," Coach Franklin said.

Cody rose from the bench. He knew it was time to take action. To rise to the occasion. To show himself to be a winner. Yes, there was a scout out there in the stands whom he could impress playing on a line with Kyle, but his dad was also out there, for the first time ever, and he didn't want to let him down. He wanted to make his dad proud.

"You don't have to tell Ryan anything," Cody said now, holding his back straight, his head up. "I'll still play on a line with him. If that's all right."

"It is," Coach Franklin said. He seemed pleased with Cody's decision.

"Then that's what I'll do," Cody said.

"Have it your way," Kyle grumbled. "It's your loss."

Kyle, Tyler, and Sean took the ice to begin the third period. Cody sat back down on the bench. He felt relieved that he'd shown the courage to do what he thought was the right thing. He looked to the stands behind the Sharks' bench and tried to make out his father. When he did, his dad smiled back at him.

Ryan approached him. "I heard you talking to Coach Franklin and Mr. Phelps," he said. "Thanks."

Cody nodded.

"And sorry for taking that crack at you the other day," Ryan added. "I was being a suck."

"Let's forget about it," Cody said.

"That's a deal," Ryan replied.
The two boys shook hands.

\*\*\*

On the ice, Kyle's anger transformed into hard-checking, frenetic hockey. Where before he had been slogged by nervousness and tension, he was now able to concentrate on the single purpose of scoring a goal.

Cody watched with avid interest, wondering how the new line would work, how Kyle would do without him. It didn't take long for Cody to get his answer. Kyle drove hard towards the Marauders' net, Tyler on his right, Sean on his left. He slipped the puck between Miles's skates and deked around Ed. Then, after a faked pass to Tyler, he charged the net like a raging bull. The goalie veered out to meet Kyle, but Kyle simply skated around him, taking a sharp turn, and, just when he was about to slip past the goal line, sent a quick wrist shot right into the empty net.

The crowd went berserk! It was a beautiful goal, a display of sheer hockey wizardry. On top of that, the score had pushed the Sharks one goal ahead of the Marauders.

A tingle of envy shot through Cody, a sense that he sure would have liked to be out there with Kyle right now, letting the cheers from the crowd wash over him, attracting the attention of the hockey scout. But he knew that he'd have his chance on the ice soon enough, and he was determined to make the most of it. When it came right down to it, he decided, he had to prove to himself that he was a good hockey player even without Kyle Kelley.

Kyle and his line took to the bench after the goal. Kyle looked at Cody. His face was full of challenge. Cody tried not to let it bother him. "Good goal," he said to Kyle.

"Thanks," Kyle answered, begrudgingly.

Cody had to move on then, past Kyle and onto the ice. He hoped that he could do something on the ice to make Kyle see that what he had done was wrong. That it wasn't fair to shove aside a player the way Kyle had done with Ryan.

Unfortunately, the Marauders' defence tightened up after Kyle's goal, and Cody and Ryan's line found it difficult to penetrate the Marauders' end. Cody could tell that Ryan was trying hard, pushing to make something happen, but there was just no give on the part of the Marauders. Cody and Ryan returned to the bench without a goal to show for their efforts.

"I really wish we could have scored," Ryan said.

"I know," Cody agreed. "We're ahead by one goal, but I still feel like, personally, I'm losing."

"That's not right. It's too bad Kyle makes us feel that way. That's what I've been trying to say all season." He looked at Cody then. "You were on the other side up to now, so I guess you didn't see it. Kyle makes you feel bad for not being as good as him."

Out on the ice, Kyle continued his scoring spree. It was as if he had been clogged up for the first two periods, and finally he had been set loose. By the time the clock showed less than two minutes left in the game, Kyle's line had racked up two more goals. The Marauders had eked out one more. The scoreboard now read SHARKS 4, MARAUDERS 2.

At the bench, Kyle sought Cody out.

"You made a mistake, buddy."

"I don't think so," Cody replied. "I think I did the right thing."

"At least we won the game," Kyle said. "I thought you were a winner before tonight, but now I'm not so sure." He stormed away down the bench, shaking his head.

"I thought you were my friend," Cody answered back, "but now *I'm* not so sure."

Kyle stopped in his tracks and turned to face Cody. For the first time Cody could remember, Kyle's face lost its confidence, its intensity. His voice trembled a bit. "I *was* your friend," he said.

"You were more interested in winning," Cody accused.

"You're right," Kyle said, and his body relaxed, as if a heavy weight were somehow lifted from his shoulders. He glanced at Ryan sitting beside Cody on the bench, then back to Cody. "But so were you." His words came out strongly, but without bitterness.

Cody didn't say a word. Kyle was right, Cody had put winning, being a hockey hero, above his friendship with Ryan. More than ever, he wanted to prove to Ryan, and even to Kyle, that he knew what being a friend was all about.

The game might as well have been over, but there were still fifty-two seconds left on the clock. Coach Franklin sent Cody, Ryan, and Noah back on the ice for the final shift of the game.

Cody was determined to make the most of it.

Noah won the face-off and immediately passed back to Lyall, who swept around a Marauders' defender and brought the puck past the centre line. Then Lyall sent the puck over to Cody, who was flying up the left side.

With the puck in tow, Cody skated forward. Out of the corner of his eye, he saw Ryan keeping pace, driving for the net. Cody stickhandled past his defender, then arced back towards the middle zone. Two Marauders were on Noah like dogs on a bone. Meanwhile, Ryan skated in closer to Cody, relatively open. Watching him, Cody was reminded of their practice games on the outdoor rink, during which they would try all sorts of plays. He wondered if one of those plays might work now. Quickly, he nudged a careful pass to Ryan and skated towards the net. Sure enough, Ryan must have been thinking of their outdoor practices as well, because he simply returned the puck to Cody for a perfect give-and-go play, one they'd practised together hundreds of times.

Now, with the puck in front of him and facing the goalie alone, Cody pushed his stick down hard on the ice and lifted the puck in a short loop over the goalie's outstretched arm and into the Marauders' net.

A goal!

There were cheers, but they didn't boom through the arena like cannon blasts. A lot of fans had already left for the evening, knowing that the Sharks were sure to win the game, hoping to beat the inevitable crush of cars in the parking lot. But that didn't matter to Cody. He knew his dad was out there, and that his dad would be even more proud of him now. The goal may not have meant much to the outcome of the game, but it meant a whole lot to Cody. And to Ryan, too.

The Sharks' players on the ice congratulated Cody and Ryan. Then the two boys congratulated themselves.

"It's a good thing you remembered that give-and-go play," Ryan pointed out.

"How could I ever forget?" Cody replied.

# 13

# A Family Reunion

Cody hurried through the automatic doors at the airport and swivelled his head this way and that, looking for his dad. Tish followed, clutching a gift she'd made in school for him to her chest. It was a shadow sketch of her profile, drawn using an overhead projector. Behind Tish, came Cody's mom, looking harried and rushed, her car keys still in her hand.

"There he is!" Tish squealed.

"Where?" Cody called out.

"Coming down the escalator!"

Cody turned and saw his father riding down the escalator, his arms loaded with gift-wrapped Christmas presents. Together, Cody and Tish ran to meet him at the bottom. Cody's mom followed them.

Setting down the gifts, Cody's dad lifted Tish into the air with one arm and perched her against his shoulder. The other arm he wrapped tenderly around Cody. "It's so good to see you guys again!"

Tish showered her dad with kisses. Cody simply enjoyed the warmth of his dad's arm around his neck.

"Hi, Phil, good to see you," Cody's mom said, nodding her head slightly.

"Hi, Janice," Cody's dad said back. "Thanks for bringing the kids."

"No problem," she said. She turned to look directly at Cody and Tish. "I'm going to drive over to Polo Park for an hour or so and then I'll be back. That'll give you plenty of time with your dad." She played with the keys in her hand.

"Please, Mom, can't you stay here with us?" Tish asked. She moved to her mom's side.

"Yeah, Mom, let's all do something together," Cody suggested excitedly. The kind of game he'd just been through, he needed the comfort of his family.

Cody's mom smiled, a thin line that just barely creased her cheeks. "No, I don't think so, guys. Your dad deserves to spend some quality time alone with you." She wiped some melting snow off her eyebrow. "But thanks for the invitation."

"Please, Mom," Tish persisted. "Let's just spend this hour together. We'll have pizza upstairs. Please!"

Cody's dad stood silent.

"No, no, it's all right," Cody's mom said, stepping back. "I have to get going or I'm liable to get a parking ticket."

Cody turned to his dad. He tugged at his sleeve. "Come on, Dad, tell her she can stay with us. That you don't mind."

Cody's dad looked at Cody's mom. He shrugged his shoulders, as if to say, What am I supposed to do? "I don't mind, Janice," he said. "You can stay. That is, if you can put up with me for an hour."

"Of course she can!" Tish offered. She was pulling on her mom's arm now. "Can't we even have one dinner together?"

Tish and Cody's mom straightened herself and put her keys away. "OK, I'll stay. You kids are really something, you know that?"

"Yahoo!" Tish cried out.

Their mom paid for one hour's worth of parking and then the four of them rode the escalator to the upper level of the airport. Cody looked around at all the people coming and going and wondered what their stories were, who they were waiting for or saying goodbye to. It was like there were so many possibilities out there, Cody thought, and you didn't really see them unless you looked really hard. He was glad about what he had decided to do at the game earlier. He felt good about it, good about himself. He had a feeling that the Transcona Sharks would be a new team come their next game. A better team.

At the pizza place upstairs, Tish got a big kick out of looking for a table for four and then the Powells went up to the counter to choose their slices of pizza. When they sat down at the table, they hung their winter coats over the backs of their chairs and started eating.

"That was a great game you played tonight, Cody," his dad told him. "And what a goal to finish things off!"

"Thanks."

"The first time I put you on skates I figured that you were made to be a hockey player," Cody's dad smiled. "It's nice to see that I was right."

Cody grinned widely and tried to keep himself from blushing. It felt good to have his dad around to tell him what a good hockey player he was.

"And don't think I didn't notice that you scored the goal on a line with Ryan Miller," Cody's mom put in. "I'm glad you two worked things out."

"So am I," Cody offered. He couldn't help feeling proud that he'd been able to score a goal without riding on Kyle's coattails.

"Isn't this great?" Tish said then, rotating her open mouth underneath a gooey string of cheese. "I wish we could do this more often."

"Well, we can't Tish, unfortunately," her mom pointed out. Her voice was strained. "As you well know, your father lives in Kamloops, and we live here."

"But he might move back," Cody put in quickly. "That could happen, right Dad?"

Cody's dad bit his lower lip. "I don't think so, kids."

Suddenly, Cody's mom's face clouded over with worry. She looked at Cody's father. "I knew this wasn't a good idea," she said.

"Don't say that, Mom," Tish objected, the crack in her voice just barely perceptible to Cody's ears. "It's so good to be together again."

Their mom hunched down then to speak to her daughter face to face. "Sweetheart, if you think that this dinner means that your father and I are getting back together again, please think again. That's not going to happen."

"How do you know?" Tish responded.

"Because, for one thing, your father has a new family of his own. For another, I would never want it."

"Mom!" Tish shouted. "If you weren't dating Coach Franklin, you wouldn't say that!"

Cody's mom shuddered. She shut her eyes tightly, not saying anything, just swaying her head back and forth.

Cody looked at his dad. His expression hadn't changed.

"Tish, my dating Joe Franklin has nothing to do with the situation between your father and me," Cody's mom said. "Your father and I couldn't live together peacefully. We had to get divorced. It was the best thing for us, and for you two."

"Your mother's right, Tish," Cody's dad added. "We're apart now because that way it's easier for everybody. I know it's difficult for you to believe that, as hard as our being apart might seem to you sometimes, but it's the truth."

Cody decided he had better say something. There were times, he had to admit, when he wished his parents would get back together, but he had accepted the fact that they never would. He had learned that it was better to make the best of what you had, than to wish for what you couldn't have. He turned to his sister. "Tish, this is a real special occasion. Let's enjoy it."

"But …"

Cody took his sister's hand. He could feel the veins on her wrist beating quickly. "Tish, this is a day you've always wished for. We're all together again. It doesn't matter how long it's going to last."

Tish remained silent. Cody could see from her face and eyes that she was struggling to make sense of his words.

"We've lost a lot lately," Cody continued, "let's not let this dinner be ruined, too."

Tish closed her eyes tightly, the way she did when it was her birthday and it was time to blow out the candles on the cake and make a wish. "You're right," she said finally. Cody could tell that she was holding back tears. "I'll be OK."

Something told Cody that his sister had just started growing up.

\*\*\*

The Powells spent the rest of the pizza dinner talking animatedly about each of their interests. Tish discussed the new karate moves she was learning, and a boy at school who was picking on her. Cody's mom talked about work, and even a little about Joe Franklin. Cody's dad talked about Della and the kids, Jeni and Cilla, who sounded a lot like Cody and Tish in many of the things they did. Cody recounted more of his hockey exploits on the Transcona Sharks.

Before any of them realized it, their time together was up. A voice over the intercom announced that Cody's dad's flight was making its last call for boarding passengers.

"I guess that's it for now," Cody's dad said, standing up. "It's been a lot of fun."

They moved together towards the departure gates, Cody holding his dad's carry-on bag while his dad gave Tish a piggyback ride. At the gate, Cody's dad put Tish down and leaned into a crouch to hug both kids at the same time.

"Goodbye, guys," he said. "Have a good Christmas."

"You, too, Dad," Cody said. He felt a tear push against his eye.

"Say hi to Jenni and Cilla for me," Tish added.

"I will," Cody's dad said. He turned to leave. Cody could tell his dad, too, was fighting back tears. It was the first time he had seen his dad like that.

"Wait, Dad!" Tish called out. "You still have a few minutes. Can you take your picture with me in that photo booth over there. I still have that one from the time you took me downtown to the Bay when I was five."

Cody's dad glanced nervously at his watch, then at the photo booth that was located about five metres away, next to a row of video games. "Tish, are you sure?"

"Please, Dad. It won't take long."

The four of them moved over to the photo booth. On its side it had a sign that read, "Four Poses, One Dollar."

Cody's mom rifled through her purse for some change. "I don't have any quarters or loonies," she said. "I'm all used up from the parking."

Cody's dad slipped his hands into his pockets, pulling out some change. Before he had a chance to count the money, Tish had lifted four quarters right out of his palm.

"We're set," she announced, leading her dad by the hand inside the booth.

Cody's dad sat down first and then Tish sat in his lap. Suddenly, though, Tish poked her head out of the black curtain draping the doorway of the photo booth.

"How about you, too, Cody?" she said.

Cody smiled. Then he looked at his mom. "I have a better idea. Why don't we all take a picture together? All four of us. One pose for each of us."

"Just take your pictures and let your dad get going," Cody's mom said sternly. "You're going to make him miss his flight."

"Come on, Mom," Cody said. "It'll be fun. We are a family, aren't we, in our own way?"

Cody's mom couldn't help breaking into a smile. "Yeah, we're a family all right." She laid her purse down next to Cody's dad's bag. "OK, move over and let me squeeze in."

Cody's mom climbed on top of Cody, who was sitting on one of his dad's knees, with Tish on the other. Then Tish poured the four quarters into the slot, and soon a red light flashed once, twice, three times, and then a fourth.

One picture for each of them, just like Tish had said.

Cody knew this was just a picture, but it would be a picture of his mom and his dad and Tish and him, together, after the divorce; it would be proof that the four of them were still a family who cared for each other, proof that in a really important way they weren't separated at all.

The pictures they were taking would be a record of a little piece of time the four of them shared together, with nobody yelling and nobody crying — all of them laughing and feeling kind of silly.

Like a family.

Cody knew that the picture would be something he was going to hold onto for a long time.

# 14

## The Sharks Regroup

The dressing room before the Transcona Sharks' practice the following Saturday was a strange place, Cody observed, as he took a locker between Ryan and Ernie. He couldn't quite put his finger on the mood that gripped the room. Coach Franklin still hadn't shown up. The players, meanwhile, were quiet, talking amongst themselves in small groups along the bench, but they had about them a nervous, fidgety air of expectation. Stick blades were being carefully retaped, hockey gloves retied, skates relaced — with more concentration devoted to each activity than should have been needed. Cody was reminded of the school gym before the first dance of the year: boys against one wall, girls against the other, and a lot of energy bouncing wildly between them. That was the way the Sharks' dressing room felt now.

At a locker further down the bench, Kyle was putting on his hockey gear, Noah helping him tie his pads.

"I saw you talking with an older guy after the last game," Noah said. "That was the hockey scout, wasn't it?"

"Yeah, it was," Kyle replied.

All the heads in the dressing room turned, Cody's included. Everybody was curious to know what the scout had told Kyle.

"So?" Noah prodded. "What'd he say?"

Kyle pulled his jersey over his head and then threw his head back to straighten his hair. "I wasn't offered a contract with the Calgary Flames, if that's what you're asking," Kyle cracked. Then his face turned serious. "Actually, that scout was a nice guy. He said I had a lot of talent and that he'd check in on me again in a few years." Kyle turned so that his eyes met Cody's. "He said I needed to stop pushing myself so hard."

"Really?" Noah looked puzzled.

"Yeah, that's what he said." Kyle didn't appear at all troubled by the information. "He said that he thought I could do it," Kyle continued, "that I could be a good playmaker if I just took some of the pressure off myself to score goals all the time. You know, give some of you guys a chance."

Cody took a step towards Kyle. It had taken a hockey scout to make Kyle realize he wasn't the only player on the team, but at least Kyle seemed to recognize it now. "I'm sure you can do it," Cody said, nodding his head. "If some of the other lines on this team start producing the way they should be, you'll have a chance to develop your playmaking skills."

"Thanks," Kyle said. Cody knew Kyle would be his friend from now on, had been his friend all along, in his own way.

People needed room to be themselves, to find out who they were and what they were capable of, Cody realized. In a way, Kyle was trapped by what his parents expected. Being a hockey hero was a box that kept Kyle from being fully himself, the same way Kyle's meanness towards Ryan had been a box around Ryan, the same way, Cody had to admit, his complaints about his mom dating Joe Franklin must have been a box around her.

When he got home later that day after the practice, he'd tell his mom that he wouldn't make a fuss again over her dating the coach. It wasn't fair to expect people to be exactly the way you wanted them to be, to put them into boxes.

"Something else that scout told me was really interesting." Kyle paused. "It's about Coach Franklin."

By now the entire team was pretty much huddled around Kyle. Everybody stopped what they were doing and waited for him to elaborate.

"The scout told me why Coach Franklin is so against rough play out on the ice," Kyle related, "and it isn't because he was hurt by someone. It's the opposite."

"What do you mean?" Lyall asked.

"Coach Franklin was what you would call a goon when he played in the IHL. He nailed a guy once in a game, and the guy nearly died." Kyle seemed to flinch at the thought. "He never played organized hockey again."

"Who?" Lyall queried. "The guy or Coach Franklin?"

"Both of them, as a matter of fact," Kyle replied. "The guy was too hurt to be any good on the ice ever again. And Coach Franklin decided he'd had enough of the game, too."

Cody nodded his head, his teeth biting his lower lip. "My dad told me the same story. I guess it's pretty much common knowledge for the people who know Coach Franklin from back in his hockey days."

"Kind of makes you understand the guy a lot better," Kyle offered.

"Sure does," Cody agreed.

"Why do you think he wouldn't tell us?" Noah conjectured.

None of the players had the chance to hazard an answer to that question. Because at just that moment, heavy footsteps echoed from the far end of the dressing room. The boys turned their heads all at once. What they saw was Coach Franklin moving towards them, his face a tangle of expressions.

"How long have you been here?" Cody asked.

"Long enough," Coach Franklin replied. "I know what you've been talking about." His tone was without accusation, as if he were somehow relieved that the truth had come out.

"Why didn't you tell us anything about what had happened to you?" Noah asked.

"There were times when I thought I should," Coach Franklin explained, his eyes glued to the boys, his hands hanging limply at his sides. "But then I'd think that I didn't want to scare any of you, that I didn't want what happened to me nineteen years ago to hang over your heads the way it's been hanging over mine for so long. This year, when I decided to coach you guys, to come back to organized hockey, I thought I could finally put that behind me. I guess I was wrong."

"I think it's best that we know," Kyle put in. "It really makes you stop and think."

"Yeah," Cody added. "Knowing what happened with you will be like a reminder to us of what can happen at any time, if we do something stupid."

Coach Franklin reached his hands out to his players, draping his huge arms around their shoulders as the boys moved in a tight circle around him. "I think maybe we're on our way to becoming a real team today, all of us," he said. "Thanks."

Suddenly, without anyone suggesting they should, the players, and Coach Franklin, joined hands in the middle of their huddle, and shouted, together, in one voice, "Sharks! Sharks! Sharks!" It was a cheer, a rallying cry, a way of showing their solidarity as a team. It was something the Transcona Sharks hadn't been able to do only a few days ago, when Mr. Phelps had asked them to.

This was a new team, a new season. Cody couldn't wait for his skates to hit the ice.

## Other books you'll enjoy in the Sports Stories series...

## Baseball

*Curve Ball* by John Danakas
*Baseball Crazy* by Martyn Godfrey

## Basketball

*Slam Dunk* by Steven Barwin and Gabriel David Tick
*Camp All-Star* by Michael Coldwell
*Fast Break* by Michael Coldwell
*Nothing but Net* by Michael Coldwell

## Figure Skating

*A Stroke of Luck* by Kathryn Ellis

## Gymnastics

*The Perfect Gymnast* by Michele Martin Bossley

## Ice hockey

*Hockey Heroes* by John Danakas
*Hockey Night in Transcona* by John Danakas
*Face Off* by Chris Forsyth
*Hat Trick* by Jacqueline Guest
*Two Minutes for Roughing* by Joseph Romain

## Riding

*Riding Scared* by Marion Crook

*Katie's Midnight Ride* by C.A. Forsyth

*A Way With Horses* by Peter McPhee

*Glory Ride* by Tamara L. Williams

## Roller hockey

*Roller Hockey Blues* by Steven Barwin and Gabriel David Tick

## Sailing

*Sink or Swim* by William Pasnak

## Soccer

*Lizzie's Soccer Showdown* by John Danakas

## Swimming

*Breathing Not Required* by Michele Martin Bossley

*Taking a Dive* by Michele Martin Bossley

*Water Fight!* By Michele Martin Bossley